Dancing
in the streets of
Brooklyn

Dancing
in the streets of
Brooklyn

April Lurie

A DELL YEARLING BOOK

Published by
Dell Yearling
an imprint of
Random House Children's Books
a division of Random House, Inc.
New York

Visit us on the Web! www.randomhouse.com/kids

Educators and librarians, for a variety of teaching tools, visit us at
www.randomhouse.com/teachers

ISBN: 0-440-41825-9

Reprinted by arrangement with Delacorte Press

Printed in the United States of America

July 2004

10 9 8 7 6 5 4 3 2 1

OPM

For my parents,
Alf and June Andersen,
and
for my husband, Ed,
with love

one

my block

Ma says it's a good thing we can't see too far down the road, 'cause we'd never take the journey. I found this true—and my journey was filled to the brim with trouble. It all started the day Jacob walked headfirst into a lamppost on my block.

"Judy's doing a dance on second base!" Harold yelled from the pitcher's mound. Second base was an imaginary square next to Mr. Johnson's front tire, and the pitcher's mound was a sewer cap. I knew it was stupid to play stickball in bare feet. It was a blistering afternoon in July, and my toes felt like sausages on a hot griddle.

"Time-out," I called to my friends. "I need shoes." I ran inside, grabbed my Keds, and plopped down on the stoop to tie my laces. Harold's Doberman pinscher, Bruiser, had been watching our game, and during this time-out he lifted his leg and christened second base.

Harold looked at me and laughed; then he scratched Bruiser behind the ear and said, "Good boy."

Great, I thought. Now I'd have to breathe hot asphalt mixed with dog pee while we finished our game. I closed my eyes for a minute and thought about the Catskill Mountains. In just a few weeks I'd be running barefoot in the cool grass and breathing in wild honeysuckle.

"Come on, Judy. We ain't got all day," Harold said. His hands were on his hips, and his jaws chomped hard on a piece of gum.

"All right, all right." I think the only reason I put up with Harold was that he let us use his Spalding ball. It was 1944, and the war was still on. Rubber was scarce and Spaldings were hard to come by.

I hopped off the porch, and that's when I saw Jacob Jacobsen walking toward us, his face turned down and his hands in his pockets. I thought it was strange for him to be coming up our street. We all knew Jacob; he was Norwegian, like us, and we saw him at school and at church. But in Bay Ridge, Brooklyn, your block was your territory—outsiders were not really welcome. If you hung out with other kids, it was on common ground like Eighth Avenue, the schoolyard, or Sunset Park.

He continued along, avoiding our stares. Annette got up to bat, and after she slammed a home run, Jacob bashed his head right into the lamppost.

We stopped our game and watched as he doubled over and let out a huge moan. I took a few steps in his direction while everyone else laughed. Jacob looked up and fixed his eyes on me. He opened his mouth to say something, but then he turned and bolted down the street.

I looked at my friends. "Gee, that's really nice," I said. "Jacob smashes his head, and you guys laugh."

"Come on, Judy, we couldn't help it," Olaf said.

Harold spit into the street. "What was he doing coming up here anyway?"

Olaf reenacted the scene. "Uh . . . which way did he go, George, which way did he go?" Then he boinked his head into an invisible pole.

"Maybe he was drunk like his old man," Harold said, pretending to put a liquor bottle to his lips.

My face burned and a lump swelled in my throat. "Shut up, Harold!" I said. "Annette, let's get out of here. I've got ten cents—I'll buy you an ice cream." I grabbed her arm and yanked her down the street. Two nickels clinked together in my pocket. I had retrieved them from the gutter that morning with a wad of old bubble gum pressed onto the end of my stickball bat. "I'm sick and tired of those boys," I said.

"Well, I don't see what the big deal was," Annette said. "It *was* kind of funny."

I looked at her and sighed. Annette and I had been best friends for most of our thirteen years, but we didn't always see eye to eye. Once, when I had spent an entire morning in Ma's little garden, sketching some lily of the valley, I picked a cluster and showed it to Annette. She said, "Yeah? Nice flowers. Come on, Judy, let's go to the schoolyard and play handball or something." I didn't bother to show her my sketch.

I thought about Jacob as we walked to the candy store. When Jacob and I were little, our mothers would meet at the ice cream parlor; they'd buy us malteds and then talk over coffee. Afterward, we would run along Eighth Avenue, jumping over cellar doors, while the two of them shopped in the Norwegian stores.

When we got older, we drifted apart. We each had our own set of friends and we didn't mix much. I knew about his father because Ma would whisper things to Pa and say what a shame it all was.

But a few months before, I'd discovered the truth about my own family. It had happened when Pa was away on his tugboat and I was snooping around in Ma's closet. Seeing Jacob made me think about this, and I didn't like it one bit. I'd been trying so hard to forget.

two

the dunking phobia

It all happened because of my sweet tooth. That's why I was in Ma's closet in the first place. I was searching for peppermints that Pa had stashed away before an earlier trip on the tugboat. I wasn't having much luck (Pa was very good at hiding things), so I started poking around at all the interesting stuff in there. That's when I came across a picture of a baby girl.

I knew the girl wasn't me—she had blond hair and I'd been born with a mop of dark curls. I searched a little further, and then I found buried underneath the picture a set of adoption papers with my name printed on each page. Pa's signature was at the bottom. It didn't make sense.

I brought the picture and the set of papers to Ma. She was in the living room, mending a pair of socks, and when she saw what was in my hands, she went pale. She put down the socks, took a deep breath, and explained it all to me.

The baby girl in the picture was my younger sister; both of us were born in Norway. My real father started drinking after I was born, and one year later, after my sister came, he abandoned us. Ma said he was an alcoholic.

After my father left us, Ma's cousin Anna, who lived in Brooklyn, sent us money to travel on a big boat to America. She'd come a few years earlier with her husband, John. They'd heard there were good jobs for Norwegians on the tugs, and Norwegian fishermen and carpenters were also being hired. Ma wanted to leave Norway; she said we needed a fresh start. And that's what we did. But my sister caught pneumonia and died on that journey. She was only six months old.

When Ma came to this point in her story, her voice got shaky and she had to stop for a few minutes. Tears dropped from her eyes, and she swallowed a few times before she could continue.

When we arrived in America, we lived with Anna and John for a while, and Ma got a job as a housekeeper. She worked for a Jewish family, and they sent her to classes at Bay Ridge High School to learn English. Soon Ma met a Norwegian seaman. They fell in love and got married, and he adopted me. That Norwegian seaman was Pa. I was too little to remember.

"You mean . . . you lied to me? All these years you lied

6

to me?" It was all I could say. Ma opened her mouth to speak, but she couldn't. She reached out her arms, but I ran to my room and slammed the door. I should have known, I thought. There were things that were different about me. My hair was dark and wavy, and my skin tanned in the summer. Roy was blond like my parents, and the three of them burned and blistered in the sun. I should have known. I wasn't Pa's daughter.

That night, Ma brought supper to my room, but I didn't eat. She told me how sorry she was, but I didn't speak. "Judy, please," she begged, "say something." But I just turned my head and shut her out.

Several times that week Ma tried to talk to me, but I refused to listen. I avoided her as much as possible, spending most of my time outside or at Annette's house. "Judy," Ma said one night at dinner, "we need to talk before Pa comes home from the boat." But I just stormed off. After a while she gave up.

The hurt ached so badly inside me that I pushed it deep down, hoping to bury it somewhere. The problem was it came out in my dreams. A faceless man with dark hair haunted me, and sometimes I was afraid to sleep. In one dream I saw the man on a big fishing boat. Ma was on the boat, too, holding her arms out to me, but she was so far away I couldn't reach her.

I dreamed of the faceless man the evening of the day Jacob walked into the lamppost. In the morning I woke up in a sweat. I got dressed, then stepped outside to check the weather.

The air was thick and hot, and Bruiser was peeing puddles up and down the street. "Roy," I called my brother through the open window. "Go get your bathing suit on." I figured we'd head over to the Sunset Park pool. It was the only way to keep from suffocating on a day like this. I also wanted to give Roy something to think about before his little brain started conjuring up new mischief.

I heard him inside the house. "Oh boy, the pool!" Pa was away on his tugboat again, towing coal up and down the coast, so I knew Roy was mine for the next couple of weeks. Ma always had chores to do, and Roy just got in her way.

I scanned our block to make sure Harold and Olaf weren't around; then I crumpled onto the stoop. Fifty-sixth Street was nothing but redbrick houses crammed together and stuck in a sea of concrete. Each lawn was a postage-stamp patch of grass that you could trim in about two minutes with a pair of toenail clippers. A big sycamore grew out of the sidewalk in front of our house, but the concrete that covered its roots seemed to be choking the life out of it. There was something choking me, too—something I needed to get away from. When Pa came home, we'd be heading for the Catskills. Normally I looked forward to this trip, but now I was dreading it at the same time.

I walked into the kitchen. Roy was running circles around Ma while she tried to pour herself a cup of coffee. He was naked except for a droopy pair of underpants with a hole in the behind. All his ribs were poking out of his skin. I figured if you hung Roy up on a pole, he'd make a pretty good skeleton for science class.

"Roy, settle down," Ma said. "Judy, be careful with him at the pool. Never take your eyes off him."

"I know, Ma, no need to worry." It seemed like I was forever telling Ma not to worry. If there was such a thing as a professional worrier, Ma would get the job hands down and we'd probably be millionaires. I poured myself a cup of coffee and sat down at the table. I'd learned to drink it bitter and black since sugar was rationed. Ma liked to save the sugar until Pa came home; then she'd make his favorites, like waffles and lingonberry cake.

Ma peered into my face. "You look tired, Judy."

"I'm all right." I lowered my head and waved her away. I knew there were dark circles under my eyes. The dream had woken me in the middle of the night, and I'd been afraid to fall back asleep. I sucked down the coffee and poured myself another cup.

Ma continued to stare, chewing the inside of her mouth. Then she set down her cup. "Well, if you're swimming today, you need to eat a good breakfast." She started pulling out pots and pans, and that's when Roy darted out the back door—underpants and all. "Roy!" she called out after him. "Come back here! You have to eat something!"

I wasn't hungry, but I choked down some breakfast to please Ma; then I did my chores. It was Wednesday, which meant scrubbing the toilet and dusting the upstairs. Roy came home and begged me to take his friend Pauley with us to the pool. It meant watching two seven-year-old babies instead of one, but I figured it would keep Roy out of my hair.

We called for Annette and Pauley and set out for the pool. When we passed the lamppost where Jacob had clonked his head, I got a sick feeling in my stomach. Bits and pieces of my dream came back to me, and I realized that Jacob had been in it. All the laughing faces from yesterday had been in it, too, and they had been laughing at me. "I'm glad we didn't run into Harold and Olaf," I said to Annette. "I don't feel like seeing them today." Annette just shrugged.

A trolley car clanked along the avenue, and swarms of people made beelines in and out of stores. We passed the Norwegian shops: the deli, the bakery, the store where Ma bought lefse and potato pancakes, and the fish store where they ground the fish into balls and cakes. On the opposite corner stood Kelly's Bar-and-Grill. The doors were open, and loud Irish music was piping out onto the street.

"Hey, Jud-aa!" Joe the Butcher yelled. He had just stepped out of his shop for a breath of fresh air. "I got something for you; come on in!"

I knew what it was—a slice of baloney. Joe had been giving me slices of baloney since I cut my two-year molars. I never had the heart to tell him I didn't like it.

The butcher shop smelled like sawdust and sharp Italian cheese. Joe stepped behind the counter, slammed down a hunk of baloney, and carved me a slice.

"Thanks, Joe." I forced a smile and took a rubbery bite. I wondered why I was always eating to please someone else.

Joe gave pieces to Annette and Pauley, but Roy clutched

his throat, gagged, and ran out the door. "That brother of yours!" Joe said. "You sure he ain't adopted or something?" Annette laughed, but I didn't. I wasn't embarrassed about Roy—I was used to that sort of thing—but what Joe had said made my heart pound, and it felt like all the blood in my body was pumping to my head. I turned away so they wouldn't see me, and I pretended to look at a salami hanging in the window.

We caught up with Roy and walked past the barber's, the shoemaker's, the grocer's, and a hundred other shops. Bay Ridge was home to a big mixture of people. Most were Norwegians, but there were a lot of Irish and Italians, too. A whole bunch of Finns lived up near Sunset Park, and we called that place Finn Town. Jews, like Mr. Titlebaum on our corner, owned the candy stores, and Germans ran most of the ice cream parlors and luncheonettes.

Pa said all these people had come to America looking for a better way of life, and when they settled here in Brooklyn, they started to build up a piece of their past. We rounded Fredheim's Restaurant. An Uncle Sam war poster hung in the window, and next to it was a sign. It read:

VE VILL VIN!
CAN YOU EVER FORGET OLD NORWAY?

At last we came to Sunset Park, and by that time we were sizzling hot. People were sprawled out around the pool, and some old Italian men were playing boccie ball in the shade of the big oak tree.

We each paid a dime to the man in the booth, and then Roy and Pauley took off. "Hey, you guys, wait up," I yelled. "We have to shower first." They didn't care—they tore off their shirts and cannonballed in. The pool was sloshing over with bodies. I saw a girl getting dunked and my palms started to sweat; the dunking phobia swallowed me whole. A few years back, a tremendous bully-kid had been dunking girls in the pool when the lifeguard wasn't looking. He had taken me by surprise and held me under for a long time. After that I barely put my head underwater. In fact, I learned how to swim freestyle by whipping my head from side to side with each stroke. Pa laughed when he saw me swim in the lake near our summer home in the Catskills; he said I looked like a crazed mule chasing a fly off its back.

Annette and I showered, jumped in, and unfortunately met up with Harold and Olaf. They were bobbing up and down, gurgling water in their mouths, and spitting it out between their teeth. I didn't want to swim with them, but Annette was already challenging Olaf to a race.

"Okay," Olaf said. "What kind of race?" He was sweet on Annette and did anything she wanted.

Harold puffed up his chest like a bullfrog. "I'll race Judy." He looked at me, eyeball to eyeball. I thought he was going to spit out a long, sticky tongue and catch a fly.

"Fine," I said. "I'll leave you in the dust."

After Annette had beaten Olaf, Harold turned to me. "Ready, Little Miss Priss?"

"Yeah, I'm ready." We took our starting positions, and on the count of three I swam my heart out. When I touched the other side of the pool and saw Harold taking his last stroke, I put my fist up in triumph.

And then came one of the most awful experiences of my life. Harold pushed my head under the water and stuck his big, ugly feet on top of my shoulders. I panicked and choked down a bucketful of water that tasted like bleach. I thought he was trying to kill me. Next thing I knew, I was hurled to the side of the pool, and when I came to my senses, I saw Jacob holding Harold by the back of his neck. "Get off me, you crazy idiot!" Harold yelled. The lifeguard blew his whistle and ordered them both out of the pool.

While Harold argued with the lifeguard, Jacob came over to where he had tossed me. I was trying to catch my breath and figure out if my brain had been damaged from lack of oxygen. "Leave me alone!" I said to him. "I can take care of myself." Jacob's wet T-shirt and shorts clung to his body, and his sneakers squished as he shifted his weight. He had jumped into the pool with his clothes on—just to rescue me.

"Are you okay?" he asked.

"Yeah, I'm fine . . . just . . . leave me alone."

Before I knew it, Jacob had hopped over the fence, jumped on his bike, and taken off dripping wet.

three
andy

I decided to find Jacob the next day. I wanted to tell him to stay away from me. Our mothers were friends, and that was bad enough. I knew what everyone said about his father being a drunk.

The truth was I didn't want to think about my own father, and when I saw Jacob that was all I could think of. I don't mean Pa, but my real father, who lived in Norway. When I saw Jacob, all the things I had ironed out in my mind got wrinkled up again.

. . .

After breakfast, Roy went to play at Pauley's house and Ma began scrubbing clothes in the bathtub. We didn't have a washing machine, but Ma was hoping to get one after the war. I slipped out the back door and got my bike from the garage. In my mind I mapped out the places I would search for Jacob.

Ma appeared in the upstairs window with a mass of perspired ringlets around her face. "*Vær forsiktig!*—Be very careful!" she called. Ma always lapsed into Norwegian when she got worked up. "And watch for cars!"

Jacob's block—Fifty-second Street—was empty, so I pedaled to the schoolyard where he sometimes played ball. Along the way I counted blue stars hanging in people's windows. Each star represented a man who was away at war. I tried not to look at the gold stars, placed there for the men who had died. I thought of Pa, and how awful it would be to have a gold star in our window instead of him. It had been almost three years since Japan bombed Pearl Harbor and the United States went to war. I prayed every day that the war would end before Pa could be drafted. They were taking the younger men first, and if they needed Pa after that, he would have to go.

When I got to the schoolyard, I saw Jacob tossing a football to Andy. Great, I thought. Great time to run into Andy. I was sweaty, probably smelly by now, red faced, and riding a bicycle made for a six-year-old. Andy was a year older than me. He had started high school the year before, so I hadn't seen him much lately, but in junior high, he had been the best athlete in school. Jacob wasn't too far behind. The funny thing about Andy was that he had a glass eye, and people said it was a miracle that he could play ball so well. I thought he was real handsome, glass eye or no glass eye, and I got jittery whenever I saw him. There was only one thing I didn't like about Andy: Jacob was his best friend.

"Hey, Judy!" Andy called, waving me over. "We were just talking about you." My arms and legs started to shake, but I managed to steer my bike over to them. Andy's hair was stringy with sweat, and his good eye was like a bright blue beacon. "Jacob and I are entering a four-man relay race at Fort Hamilton, and we need two more kids for our team. Can you and Annette run with us?"

My eyes went wide. "Did you say a four-*man* relay race? Annette and I are girls."

The two of them laughed. "I *know* you're girls," Andy said. "It's just *called* a four-man relay. I don't think any other girls are racing, but there's no rule against them— we checked."

I could feel my face getting hot. How could I have said something so stupid? I was curious about the race, but I wanted to melt into the ground at the same time.

"Jacob told me how good you ran in school last year," Andy said. "You and Annette had the best times for the quarter mile. So, what do you say?"

"Well . . ." This was happening so fast. What Andy said was true—Annette and I could beat just about anyone—but did I really want to run in a race with Jacob? He was the kid I was trying to get rid of.

"We're gonna train every morning at the high school," Andy continued, "and the race is two weeks from this Saturday. How about if you guys meet us at the track tomorrow, say nine o'clock?"

I realized I couldn't say no. This was something big—an official race against boys—and I knew Annette would be thrilled. "Okay," I said. "I guess we'll do it."

"Great," Andy said.

I looked at Jacob. I squeezed my handlebars and took a deep breath. I had to get this over with. "Listen, Jacob," I said, "thanks for helping me at the pool the other day. I mean, you practically saved my life, but now . . . could you just leave me alone? Really, I can handle things by myself."

Jacob blinked a few times, then lowered his head. I saw one corner of his mouth turn up.

Andy elbowed him. "Hey, what's this about?"

Jacob didn't say anything. Instead, he looked at me, like I should answer the question. I thought I'd be better off if a truck ran me over.

Andy laughed out loud and tossed the football to Jacob. "I gotta hear about this," he said. "See you tomorrow, Judy. Nine o'clock—don't be late."

I pedaled home on Jell-O legs. My heart was thumping away inside my chest. I'd made such a fool of myself, it was too painful to think about. And now I was going to have to see Jacob every day for the next couple of weeks. But I'd be seeing Andy, too. I'd be running with Andy—and Andy thought I was fast. I wondered if he thought anything else about me.

As I rode up our block, I saw Harold walking out his front door. He charged into the street, waving his arms. "Judy, hold on!" he yelled.

I tried to dodge him, but he grabbed the handlebars of my bike and straddled the front tire. "Hey, look," he said, "I didn't mean it, okay? I forgot that you're afraid to put your head underwater."

I folded my arms across my chest and glared at him. He had a crooked grin that reminded me of how he had looked when he tried to kiss me in the coat closet in sixth grade. Since then, it seemed like there had always been tension between us.

"So . . . what's the deal?" he said. "Is Jacob your boyfriend or something?"

"Of course not." I decided not to mention anything about Jacob, Andy, and the relay race.

"All right then," he said. "Are we friends again?"

"Yeah, I guess so. Now move out of the way, Harold, will you? I'm going to Annette's."

Harold let go of the handlebars and watched me ride up the street. "You swam pretty good in that race," he called out, "but I'll get you next time!"

four

squeezes

I had trouble falling asleep that night. I kept thinking about my conversation with Andy and how ridiculous I'd sounded. I stared at the ceiling and rehearsed intelligent phrases to use the next day.

After that, I counted the days on my fingers to see if Pa would be home in time for the race. He would. I knew he'd like to see me run; it was the kind of thing he'd get real excited about. But lately, when I thought about Pa, I felt so jumbled inside.

Things were really bad when he first came back from the boat, right after I'd found my adoption papers. I remembered his voice booming through the front door, "I'm home!"

It was a rainy afternoon in May, and I was in my room finishing some homework. He'd been out at sea for three weeks, and normally I'd run down to greet him. Instead I hopped into bed and pulled up the covers. I wondered if Ma was going to tell him what had happened. I hoped not, but deep down I knew she would. She never kept secrets from Pa. Just me, it seemed.

I heard Roy barrel across the living room to give him a big hug, but after a minute Pa was calling me. "Judy! Where's my girl? Come on, I want my squeeze!"

A "squeeze" was the type of hug that Pa gave me and Roy when he came back from the boat. He'd have a faceful of blond stubble—"Why should I shave out at sea when there's no one to look handsome for?" he'd say—and before Ma could order him to the bathroom to take off his whiskers, he'd grab us and rub his chin on the tops of our heads and across our cheeks. This would set us off laughing, and Pa thought it was great fun.

"Judy!" he called again. I didn't budge. "Judy!" I heard him bounding up the stairs. I shut my eyes tight.

He pushed my door open. "You're sleeping? What's the matter, are you sick?" He sat down on the edge of my bed and reached out to touch my forehead, but I turned away.

"You should knock first," I said. "I'm thirteen years old, Pa."

Pa was silent for a minute. "You're right, Judy. I'm sorry. I'll knock from now on. I was just looking forward to seeing you."

I turned and looked at him. "And I'm too old for a squeeze."

"Oh. Okay. How about just a hug?"

Reluctantly, I put my arms around him. "That's more like it," he said.

"I'm not feeling good, Pa. I just want to rest."

He looked at me in a funny way; then nodded slowly, got up, and headed downstairs. I lay there, listening to him and Roy laugh and swap stories in the kitchen while Ma fixed them something to eat.

The next day, Pa was real quiet, and I figured Ma had told him. I caught him glancing at me a few times, about to speak, then biting his lip and holding back. Neither of us knew what to say. Ma busied herself around the house, but she kept stopping to sigh and stare at the walls. That night, she fixed my favorite dinner—Norwegian meatballs—but no one talked much during the meal.

I watched Pa and Roy that evening as they played together so easily, and I wondered if Pa loved Roy more than he loved me. I thought he must. Roy was his real child, his flesh-and-blood child. I wondered, too, about my little sister. I didn't even know her name. Was she buried somewhere, or did her body have to be thrown off the side of that boat? And my real father—how could he have done such a rotten thing? I hated him for drinking, hated him for leaving us.

I was pretty miserable the next few days. Then one night, Pa knocked on my door while I was studying. "Can I talk to you, Judy?"

My stomach tightened. "I'm kind of busy, Pa. I've got a big test in the morning."

"It'll only take a minute."

I took a deep breath and braced myself. "Okay."

He opened the door slowly and sat down across from me. I'd never seen him look so nervous. "Ma told me what happened," he said. "I'm sorry you had to find out that way, Judy."

A big lump started to form in the back of my throat.

"Ma told me she's been trying to talk to you."

I shrugged and looked away.

"I understand how you feel, Judy, but back then, we were told to keep everything a secret. We thought it would be better if you didn't know." Pa hung his head. "Now I can see we made a big mistake."

I glanced at Pa and swallowed hard.

He sighed deeply. "I've been thinking about this for a while," he said, "and I thought if I told you a story about myself, it would help you understand some things."

I wondered how a story about Pa could have anything to do with how I felt. But I nodded and said, "Okay."

"Well, when I was fourteen," he began, "just a year older than you, times were very hard in Norway. I had to leave my family and go out to sea."

My eyes opened wide. "But how could your parents just let you go?"

"They didn't have much choice," he said. "I was the oldest of nine children, and there wasn't enough food to go around, so I got work on a Norwegian freighter. I stayed on for four years, and then, when I was eighteen, I jumped ship in the New York Harbor. I had heard there was work on the yachts—up on City Island in the Bronx—so I went. I didn't know anyone, and I had no place to stay. I slept in the park for three nights. Luckily, after that, someone hired me."

I couldn't believe this about Pa. I couldn't imagine him sleeping on a park bench like a hobo. "How come you never told me this before?"

He smiled, but his face didn't look happy. "It's what I've been trying to explain to you. You see, us Norwegians, we don't like to talk about painful things. We're known to be pretty closemouthed, and it's hard for us to say how we feel. It has to do with the way we were brought up."

This was something I knew, even though it had never been explained to me before. I thought of the Ole and Lena jokes that Norwegian people told. One of them went like this: Ole loved Lena so much, he *almost* told her.

"But I didn't finish the story," Pa said. "Years later, after working on the yachts, I got a job on the tugboats. That's when I met your mother. And you, too. But Ma told you this part already, didn't she?" Pa waited for me to say something, but I couldn't speak. He took my hand. "I've always loved you like my own daughter, Judy. I don't want this to change things between us."

I let those words sink in. I still felt awful, but what Pa said helped a little.

"I want you to understand how Ma feels, too," he went on. "She's been through a lot, and this has been really hard for her. She can barely talk about what happened to her in

23

Norway and on the boat coming here. I don't think she's even told me everything."

I thought about Ma and felt ashamed of how I'd been treating her.

"I know you need time," Pa continued. "These things take time, and that's okay." He stroked my head for a while, then got up to leave.

When he reached the door, I said, "Pa, wait. You didn't tell Roy anything, did you?"

"No, Roy doesn't know."

"Please don't tell him."

"Okay, I won't."

Pa walked out, and I thought about what he had said. I knew it was true, that I needed time, but I didn't want to talk about these things anymore. Not now, not later. I just wanted to move on.

But now, as I lay there in bed remembering all this, I realized that a few months had gone by and there were still many unanswered questions. I knew Ma was waiting for me to come to her, but I wasn't ready to hear what she had to say. I wondered if I'd ever be ready and if I'd ever feel right again. Finally I got sleepy, so I closed my eyes. I was glad to have the race to think about. I would concentrate on that, on the training, and take one day at a time.

five

boyfriend?

Annette was waiting for me on her stoop when I left my house the next morning. She was really charged up. "I still can't believe it," she said as we walked to the high school. "We're finally getting to run in a real race against boys."

"Yeah, but let's be calm about this whole thing, okay? I don't want to stand out."

"Judy, we're the only girls competing. How could we *not* stand out?"

She had a point.

At the school, a sea of bodies—bending, flexing, and loosening tight hamstrings—covered the field.

"Judy, look, there's Andy and Jacob. They're waving us over," Annette said.

Andy's face was tight and serious; he knew the competition was tough. As we trekked across the field, we heard a variety of snorts and snickers and felt a thousand eyes on us. One skinny kid gawked at me, and I wanted to reach out and choke him.

Then I heard Annette's voice. "What are you staring at, you morons?" She was mouthing off at some rough-looking boys.

I grabbed her arm and pulled her along. "Cut it out!" I said. "What are you trying to do, get us killed?"

"We'll show them," she said. "Wait till they see us win this race."

I peeked behind me. One of the boys gave me an evil smile and bashed his fist into his palm. I just wanted to survive.

Andy put us right to work; he had organized a complete training program. First we stretched; then we did push-ups, sit-ups, leg lifts, and knee bends. Jacob kept craning his neck over to me, making comments and trying to be friendly, but I ignored him as best as I could. When he looked at me, I looked the other way. When he spoke to me, I answered in as few syllables as possible.

After the warm-up, we did some sprints around the track, and Andy was amazed at our speed. "Jacob was right," he said. "You girls are like lightning, even better than I expected."

We finished our practice with a five-mile run along the

bay on Shore Road. It was a beautiful morning. The water was calm, and the sun glimmered specks of light on a big red tugboat. Andy and Annette were running ahead of me in the distance, and Jacob was trailing behind me. I waved to the tug, just in case it was Pa's boat, and then a sad feeling swept over me. I remembered the last time I had waved to a tug. I was with Roy, eating ice cream on the Sixty-ninth Street pier. When we spotted the boat, we jumped up and down, waved our ice cream cones in the air, and called, "Pa! Pa!" I felt wonderful and proud that my father was a tugboat captain. That was before I knew the truth. It was all so easy then.

After a while, Jacob came alongside me, huffing and puffing. "You don't feel it at all, do you?" he said.

"Feel what?"

"You know—the running. Look at me. I'm already out of breath."

"Oh . . . yeah." I tried to speed up a bit, but he hung right in there.

"You're amazing," he said.

"No, I'm not." I tried to lose him again, but he wasn't taking the hint.

Andy and Annette turned around at the two-and-a-half-mile point and headed back to Fort Hamilton; we followed their lead. I didn't feel like talking to Jacob, but since we were running and I couldn't get rid of him, I decided to ask a question. "Hey, Jacob," I said. "The other day, when you came up our block and smashed your head on the pole, what did you want?"

"Oh," he said. "I was hoping you'd forget about that. I

was gonna ask you about the race that day, but instead I wound up with a cracked head."

I looked at him and laughed. "Well, maybe you should watch where you're going from now on."

"Yeah, maybe. But you know what I think? I think you should watch out for Harold."

I scrunched up my face. "Harold? I'm not worried about him."

"He's not your boyfriend, is he?"

"Boyfriend? Are you kidding? If I had a boyfriend, it sure wouldn't be a kid who dunks my head underwater!"

"Okay," Jacob said, holding up both hands and laughing. "I was just wondering."

"And that's another thing," I said. "What were you doing that day at the pool, anyway?"

"Saving your life, remember?"

"Oh, very funny. And I told you before, I can take care of myself!" I took off in a full sprint ahead of him. That kid was becoming a royal pain in the neck.

six

next stop, coney island

Back at the field we cooled down and stretched our tight muscles. Andy had us sit in the grass with the soles of our feet together. While we bounced our knees, he gave us a pep talk. "Okay, that was good for the first day. If we want to win, we've got to be tough and train hard."

"We're *going* to win," Annette said. She stuck her nose in the air, then plunged her forehead to the tips of her toes.

"That's good," Andy said. "A positive attitude really helps."

Annette raised her head and smiled at Andy. They bounced knees in unison. I rolled my eyeballs and Jacob caught me. He started to smile, but I quickly turned away.

We got drinks at the water fountain and headed home. The sidewalk was too narrow for the four of us, so we walked two by two—Andy and Jacob ahead, Annette and me behind. While Annette chattered into my ear, I studied the boys closely.

Andy's platinum hair hung past his ears, and it looked like silk blowing in the breeze. His shoulders stood broad above his wiry body, and his arms and legs were smudged with bits of dirt. His Keds were beat up, and his dungaree shorts were baggy and frayed.

Jacob was the complete opposite. His clothes were crisp and new, his Keds were white, and it looked like he had just stepped out of a barber shop. Andy had muscles; Jacob was just plain skinny.

Jacob turned around and flashed his eyes at Annette and me. "Just making sure you girls don't disappear," he said.

Andy had to run an errand for his mother, so he said good-bye to us when we reached Sixtieth Street. "Nine A.M. *sharp*!" he called out as he made his way to the grocer.

Now it was just the three of us. Annette had lots of nonsense to talk about until we came to our corner. "Well, see you tomorrow, Jacob," she said.

"You can't get rid of me that fast," he said. "I'm walking you girls home."

"My, what a gentleman," Annette said, raising her eyebrows at me. I just cleared my throat and squinted up the block. I could see Harold and Olaf playing ball in the distance. We stopped in front of Annette's house. "Hey," I said to Annette, "I promised Roy I'd take him to Coney Island this afternoon. Can you come? We're gonna buy tickets for Steeplechase and do all the rides."

Annette groaned. "I wish I could, but I have to baby-sit my little cousin."

"Aw, come on, can't you get out of it?"

"No, not this time. But call me when you get back." She climbed her front stairs and turned around. "Bye, Jacob. Thanks for the walk home." She raised her eyebrows at me again, then disappeared through her front door.

"See you tomorrow, Jacob," I said. I scooted up the block, hoping he'd walk the other way. No such luck.

"I'll walk you to your house," he said, catching up to me. "I'd like to see Roy, anyway."

"Roy?" I looked at him like he was crazy. "Why would you want to see Roy?"

"He was my little brother in Boy Scouts. We worked on some projects together at church. We built a pretty nice go-cart."

I glanced up the street. I saw Harold wave good-bye to Olaf, and then he headed our way. He tossed his Spalding ball high above his head, then reached up and caught it. That's when he saw us. His eyes narrowed into slits and his jaw jutted out.

Roy flew out our front door before Harold reached us. "Judy! I've been waiting for you. What took you so long? Ma packed us a lunch, and I'm all ready to go." When he saw Jacob, his eyes nearly popped out of his skull. "Jacob! Is that you?"

"Hey, Roy!" Jacob held his arms out to him.

"You came to see me!" Roy ran to him and plastered his arms around Jacob's waist.

"Yeah, that's right." He picked Roy up and twirled his puny body around like it was made of paper.

"So, you're coming with us to Coney Island. This is great!" Roy beamed at me. "Thanks for a great surprise, Judy. I'll tell Ma, and she'll pack another lunch." Roy flew back into the house.

"Roy, wait a minute!" I yelled, but it was too late. I turned to Jacob. "I'm sorry. You don't have to come." Please don't come, I thought.

"Why should you be sorry? Besides, maybe I *want* to go. And I certainly wouldn't want to disappoint Roy."

I folded my arms across my chest.

Roy barreled out the door again, this time dragging Ma along. "See, Ma, there he is. Judy brought him to see me."

"Hello, Jacob," Ma said. She stumbled down the stairs with a big lunch bag in her arms. She didn't notice Harold, who was just a stone's throw away now.

"Hi, Mrs. Strand," Jacob said.

"How's your mother?"

"Oh, she's fine."

Harold stepped right up to Jacob, spit over his shoulder, and looked him square in the face. Jacob held out his hand to Harold, and since Ma was standing right there, Harold didn't have much choice; he took it. They shook hands, squeezing hard until their fingers turned purple.

Ma cleared her throat. "Jacob, I'm glad you're going to

32

Coney Island with Roy and Judy. Sometimes I worry about them when they go off on their own."

"What are you talking about?" I said. "I'm perfectly capable of taking care of myself and Roy!"

Jacob said, "Don't worry, Mrs. Strand. I'll take good care of them."

I threw my hands up in the air.

"Here's your lunch," Ma said, handing me the heavy bag. "I hope it's enough."

Jacob said, "Thank you, Mrs. Strand. We'll be home before dark." Then he turned to Harold and said, "See ya later, Harold." Roy grabbed Jacob's arm and tugged him along. Harold just stood there with a peculiar look on his face.

As we walked to the train station, the two Boy Scout buddies jabbered on and on about the pinewood derby that was coming up. Jacob was giving Roy all kinds of advice on how to build his race car. Roy's fickle little brain seemed to have lapsed into a coma, because he asked Jacob to help him build it. I had already promised to help him. I looked at Jacob and wondered if anyone had actually *invited* him to come with us. I cleared my throat and said, "Jacob, don't you need to tell your folks where you're going?"

"Nope," he said. "They don't worry about me. Hey, I'll race you to the train station. Whoever gets there first puts in the nickels."

I was *not* going to let him pay my fare. I tossed the lunch bag to Roy and he almost toppled over. "No fair!" I yelled as I took off. "You got a head start!" When Jacob reached the station, he dug into his pocket, pulled out three nickels, and dropped them into the slots of three turnstiles. When I caught up to him, I scowled and said, "Why'd you do that?"

" 'Cause I wanted to," he said with a big grin.

"Okay, Mr. Big-time Spender, I'm buying you an orangeade when we get there."

"No, you won't. I invited myself today, so it's my treat."

"Oh yeah? We'll see about that."

When Roy caught up to us, we heard the train thundering underground, so we pushed through the turnstiles and galloped down the stairs. The train came to a screeching halt; then the doors opened wide and we hopped on. Jacob sat between me and Roy with his leg pressed against mine, and as I inched my leg away, he pressed his leg closer. I pretended not to notice. When the conductor said, "Next stop, Coooooney Island," I stood up. I couldn't take it anymore. I was all sweaty and flustered. The doors opened and Roy ran onto the elevated platform.

"Roy! Wait up!" I yelled.

"It's okay, Judy," Jacob said. "I'll keep an eye on him."

"Oh, that's right, I forgot. Mr. Wonderful is here."

My eyes darted around looking for Roy; then I spotted him. He was talking to a raggedy-looking lady who was sitting on a bench with two skinny little kids. He plopped our lunch on the lady's lap and took off again.

"Roy!" I yelled. "What are you doing?" I ran after him and grabbed him by the back of his shirt. Ma had scraped together enough money for me and Roy to get into Steeplechase; we didn't have anything extra for food.

Jacob came running up behind us. "Judy, it's okay. I have money for lunch." I looked back at the woman and her kids; they were already opening the bag of food, and they looked hungry. "Come on," he said, "we'll go to Nathan's."

When I heard that, my mouth started to water like a spring. I let go of Roy's shirt.

"Thanks, Jacob!" Roy said. Then he ran toward the subway stairs, boxing with his fists in the air and yelling, "Nathaaaaan's!"

seven

the cyclone

We gulped down cold sodas and feasted on frankfurters and French fries. "I wish we could eat *this* every day," Roy said. "Ma makes us eat stuff like fish pudding and turnips." He crinkled his nose and shuddered.

"Yeah," Jacob said, smiling. "And how about *lapskaus*?"

"Oh, that's the worst," I said. *Lapskaus* was a thick Norwegian stew with all the leftovers thrown in. Ma made it whenever she cleaned out the icebox.

"No," Roy said. "*I* know what the worst is. Lutefisk."

We all agreed. Dried codfish soaked in lye looked and smelled so nasty that only the adults would eat it. Pa said lutefisk kept the Vikings alive on their expeditions. He was always bragging about the Vikings.

I watched Jacob chug the rest of his soda. He popped the last bit of frankfurter into his mouth. I started to wonder where he got all his money and why he was so free to spend it.

"So, Jacob," I said. "Where'd you get all this cash? I didn't know you were rich."

He shook his head. "I'm not rich."

Roy piped up. "Well, you're richer than we are. Sometimes Judy and I have to pull up change from the gutter if we want an ice cream or a candy."

My cheeks started to burn. I wanted to pop Roy on the back of his head, but instead I looked down at the greasy table.

"My father just had a run of luck on his fishing boat," Jacob said, "so he gave me some extra money this week. Believe me, sometimes I got nothing." Jacob frowned and looked away. It seemed like he was remembering something. Then he patted Roy's shoulder. "Come on, let's go down to the beach for a while. We gotta let our food digest before we ride the Cyclone."

Roy grabbed the rest of his French fries and we headed out the door. He stuffed some into his mouth as we were walking and said, "Judy won't ride the Cyclone."

"Oh no?" Jacob said. He looked at me and laughed.

I turned to Roy. "Says who, smarty-pants?"

"Says you," Roy said with his mouth full, spitting pieces

of French fries into the air. "When Pa took us last year, you waited for us at the exit gate—shakin' in your boots."

"That was last year," I said. The two of them laughed at me, so I walked on ahead. I remembered the story Harold had told me about that roller coaster, and it made my head spin. A girl with long hair, down to her knees, rode the Cyclone on a windy day, and after she came down the first hill, her hair flew up and got caught in the tracks above her head. She was yanked out of her seat and left dangling in midair. When I told Pa the story, he said it was a bunch of baloney, but I wasn't so sure. Anyway, I was glad I had tied my hair up that day.

The ocean was blue-green, and the waves sprayed bits of white foam. I sat down and breathed in the salty air; it was a glorious afternoon. I kicked off my shoes and buried my feet in the sand. Jacob and Roy ran down to test the water.

Roy squealed as Jacob splashed him along the shore. After a while, Jacob came and sat down next to me. We watched Roy jump the waves and collect shells. When he found a shell he liked, he stuffed it in his pocket. "Roy's a great kid," Jacob said. He buried his feet next to mine.

"Oh yeah," I said, "what a kid."

Jacob smiled at me, and my stomach did a little flip. I leaned forward and scribbled designs in the sand with my fingers. I wasn't sure whether I liked being this close to him. I had an urge to get up and run, but a tiny piece of me wanted to stay.

"Hey, look at those big fishing boats," Jacob said, pointing way offshore.

I looked at the boats in the distance and thought about the time Pa had taken me out on his tugboat. I remembered gripping the side rails as the water churned beneath me. Pa had put his arm around me so I'd feel safe. "Did you ever go out fishing on your father's boat?" I asked.

"No." Jacob frowned and stabbed a piece of driftwood into the sand. "He says I'm still too young. My brother Peter used to fish with him, but Peter's in the war now. He's the chief engineer on a ship in the Pacific."

"My mother told me about that," I said. "You must be proud of him."

"I am." Jacob squinted across the water. "Andy's father is in the war, too," he said, "and it's really hard 'cause Andy's got three little brothers. He's got to help his mother all the time."

"Wow." I thought about Andy and how lonely he must be without his father. "I bet Andy really misses him."

"He does."

I hugged my knees to my chest. "I guess I'm lucky in a way. I don't have any family in the war."

"That *is* lucky," Jacob said. "You know my sisters, Ingrid and Aslaug?"

I nodded, remembering that Jacob had two married sisters.

"Well, both their husbands are stationed over in Europe now."

"Really? I didn't know that."

"Yeah, so Ingrid and Aslaug had to move in together. They both work downtown, in one of those factories where they make the war machinery."

I pictured two ladies in baggy overalls, flexing their biceps like Rosie the Riveter. I scooped up some sand, held it in my palms, and thought for a while. "That must be strange," I said, "having two sisters who are already married."

"Yep . . . I'm the big accident."

I looked at him. "What do you mean?"

"*Accident* . . . You know . . . they weren't planning on having another kid. I came ten years after my brother Peter."

"Oh," I said so quietly it was almost a whisper. I let the sand run through my fingers. Ma had given me a book about sex, which I had painfully read, but I wasn't quite sure how accidents happened. "Well, your life is no accident," I said, hoping to end it there.

Jacob smiled to himself as if he knew better. We sat for a while, watching the seagulls swoop down on some food, and I started to think about my real father. I began to wonder if *I* was an accident. Maybe he never wanted me in the first place. Maybe that's why he started drinking. Maybe that's why he left—because he never wanted me or my sister.

"Hey, let's go," Jacob said. He grabbed my hand and helped me to my feet; then he grinned. "I want to see you ride the Cyclone."

"Very funny."

Jacob whistled and Roy came running up from the shore. We headed to the boardwalk.

eight

stuffed turtle

We strolled along the Coney Island boardwalk, taking in all the sights. Sandy, sunburned kids rinsed their feet in the showers while beer-drinking men tried their luck at the roulette wheels. Young girls walked arm in arm with soldiers and sailors on furlough. There were so many smells floating in the air: steamed crabs, knishes, popcorn, and beer.

Benny Goodman, the King of Swing, played over the loudspeakers, and we stopped to watch some kids practice the lindy. It looked like fun, but Norwegian Lutherans—at least all the ones I knew—weren't allowed to dance. One time Pauley's sixteen-year-old brother, Joseph, was desperate for a date for his high school dance and he asked me to go.

(Joseph and Pauley were Irish Catholics.) I told him I'd have to check with my mother, but I already knew what the answer would be. Ma nearly fell over when I mentioned it. "We don't dance, Judy; you know that," she said. I had to tell Joseph no, and boy, was he mad. He couldn't even get a date with a thirteen-year-old.

We stood there on the boardwalk, and I watched Jacob tap his toes to the beat of the music. I wondered what it would be like to dance the lindy with him.

Roy peeled off his wet T-shirt and swung it back and forth as we continued to walk. His pockets were so jam-packed with shells they were making his shorts droop, exposing a good portion of his underwear. Two teenage girls in bathing suits laughed and pointed at Roy. One said, "Look at that muscle man!" The other one put her hand to her heart and swooned. Roy didn't notice. He *did* look pitiful. I couldn't blame them for laughing. I trotted a pace ahead to avoid the embarrassment.

When we reached Steeplechase, I told Roy to dump the shells out of his pockets; he was a mule. "No!" he said. "I wanna keep them *all*. You can't make me."

"Roy," Jacob said, "the shells could fall out on the rides and hit people on the head. They might throw us out of the park. You wouldn't want that to happen, would you?"

"I didn't think of that," Roy said. He emptied his pockets halfway. Jacob winked at me like he had everything under control. I wanted to sock him.

We made our way to the ticket booth, and while I

wasn't looking, Jacob bought three tickets. I got so mad I shoved him and threw my money at him. I tried to rip up the ticket, but he snatched it out of my hand and dragged me into the park. Roy scooped up the coins and stuck them back in my pocket. I was rip-roaring mad.

We went on every ride in Steeplechase, and then Jacob took us on the Cyclone. I rode that stupid roller coaster five times. The funny thing was when it was time to leave, I was disappointed. The afternoon had passed so quickly.

We tramped back along the boardwalk, past the game booths and penny arcades. Jacob and Roy stopped to watch a baseball-pitching game, so I slipped away and bought three frozen custards with the money Ma had given me. When I returned, Roy was jumping up and down with a stuffed turtle in his arms.

"Judy! Look what Jacob won for you! He pitched the baseball right at the target."

"What?"

"Jacob won this for you. I told him you like turtles, so he chose this one. Isn't it great?"

"I don't want it! I'm too old for stuffed animals, any-way—especially turtles!" I handed each of them a frozen custard and turned around in a huff.

"Thanks," Jacob said. "I love custard." I peeked over my shoulder and watched him bite the curlicue off the top.

Roy tried to shove the turtle into my arms, but I pushed it away and it fell to the ground. Jacob picked it up and tried to hand it to me; he looked a little frightened.

"Give it to Roy!" I said. "I told you, I'm too old for stuffed animals!" I marched ahead of them, eating my custard, but it tasted more like cold, wet cardboard.

By the time we got off the train, dusk was setting in. Ma would be happy to see us home before dark. We walked along the avenue, and right before we came to our corner, we saw Douglas O'Reilly and his henchmen advancing toward us. As usual, they were looking for any trouble they could find. Douglas's father owned one of the bars on Eighth Avenue. "Let's cross over," I said. "I don't feel like walking past the imbeciles."

Jacob's face grew serious and his shoulders tightened. "Yeah, good idea."

"I ain't afraid of those creeps," Roy said. "Why should we have to move because of them?"

I yanked him along. "Just do it, Roy." As we crossed the avenue, Douglas and his gang crossed, too.

One of the gang yelled out, "Look! A bunch of stupid squareheads." Now, it was okay for a Norwegian to joke around and call himself a squarehead, but when someone Irish said it, there was bound to be trouble.

"Micks!" Roy called back.

"Shut up, punk!"

"Roy, cut it out!" I said. I braced myself and prayed for help.

"Hey!" Douglas shouted. "If it isn't Jacob Jacobsen. And who's he got with him? Oh! It's Miss Goody Two-shoes and her ugly-faced brother."

"If you've got something to say, you say it to *me*!" Jacob shouted. His voice made me jump out of my skin.

"Yeah, I do have something to say to you, Jacobsen. Your father was in our bar last night, drunk as a skunk and makin' a damn fool of himself. Couldn't even find his way to the john. We all had a good laugh when your mother had to come in and drag him home."

A deep animal sound came from Jacob's throat. His neck looked like a bundle of ropes. He charged at Douglas with all his might and walloped him right in the face. Douglas plunked to the ground with blood spurting out of his nose. Then the rest of the gang pounced on Jacob. My prayers were answered just in time, because when I looked up our street, I saw Harold and his older brother, Steve. Steve was big and strong, and tough as nails. Their dog, Bruiser, was right by Harold's side.

"Harold! Steve!" I called. They bolted down the street with Bruiser in the lead. The gang scattered like a bunch of cockroaches, leaving Jacob and Douglas on the sidewalk. They both had bloody noses, and Jacob had a fat lip.

"You bunch o' cowards!" Harold yelled after them. Then he knelt next to Jacob.

Steve looked angry. He grabbed Douglas by his shirt collar, and Bruiser growled, low and deep. It scared *me* clear out of my mind, but Douglas barely flinched. "You stay away from here, you piece of scum!" Steve yelled. Then he threw Douglas aside. Bruiser was snarling and showing his teeth.

Douglas raised his fist. "I'll get you back for this, Jacobsen."

"You're a piece of trash, O'Reilly," Harold said. "Get outta here before I sic my dog on you." Bruiser's jaws started snapping, so Douglas ran. Harold put his arm around Jacob and helped him up. "Come on, Jacob," he said. "Let's get you cleaned up. You need some ice for that lip, too." Harold gave Bruiser a few love pats and said, "Good boy!"

Roy and I hadn't moved the entire time. We just stood there, our mouths like two O's. Then Roy took my hand and pulled me over to Jacob, but Jacob wouldn't look at us. He was breathing hard and holding his side. We walked up the block in silence. Harold took Jacob to his house, and I took Roy home.

That night, before I went to sleep, Ma came to my room and knocked on the door. She was really concerned about Jacob; she'd been talking to his mother on the phone. "Judy, can I come in?"

"Yes, Ma, it's open."

I was sitting on my bed, looking out the window. Ma sat down next to me. "Are you okay?" she asked.

"Yeah, I guess so. Just a little shaken up."

"Those boys have started so much trouble around here," Ma said, shaking her head. "If you see them again, if they do anything else, I want to know right away."

I nodded. "Okay."

Ma sat there quietly, and after a while I noticed she was breathing a little heavy. "Judy?"

I turned to her.

"Pa will be home in time to see the race," she said.

"I know."

"He's going to be very excited."

I smiled halfway and nodded.

"I hope," Ma said, and then hesitated. "I hope this time will be different—for you and Pa. Maybe you can give him a hug when he comes home, tell him what you've been doing, how you've been training. He'd really like that."

I lowered my eyes. I knew that hugging Pa and telling him about the race would be difficult. Nothing like that was easy anymore.

Ma sat there awhile longer. "There's something I've been wanting to give you, Judy," she said. "And I think now is a good time."

I wondered what it was and I felt nervous. "Really?" I said. "What is it?"

"Wait here," Ma said. "It's in my room." Ma left and came back a minute later, holding a small box. She sat down and placed it in my hands. "Please, open it."

Slowly, I lifted the top of the box. Inside was the picture of my baby sister, the one I'd found with my adoption papers. Ma had framed it.

"Her name was Pearl," Ma said softly.

"Oh." I thought it was a beautiful name, although I didn't say this to Ma.

"I don't have a picture of your father," she said, "and I'm sorry for that. When I left Norway, I was too angry. I thought I could just forget everything—start over. I found out later that I was wrong."

I was only half listening to what Ma was saying. I ran my finger over the frame. It looked expensive. I wanted Ma to leave; I wanted to be alone with the picture.

"I wish I had something else to give you," she said.

I shook my head. "I don't need anything."

Ma sighed. "Judy, I don't want you to be angry and hold things in. I did that for so long, and in the end it hurt me so much. I wish you would talk to me."

I squeezed my eyes shut. "I can't, Ma. I can't talk about anything now."

She reached out and pulled my head gently to her chest. My body was stiff, and I couldn't relax. "Okay, Judy," she said. "When you're ready, then." She kissed my cheek and said good night.

I stared out my window, holding the picture to my chest. There must have been a full moon, because the back-yard was dimly lit and I could see two cats sitting outside our garage. I got up slowly and took a few steps toward my desk. I studied the photograph for a while, tracing the outline of the baby's face. "Pearl," I whispered. I noticed that the back of the frame had a pop-out stand so I could place it upright on my desk if I wanted to. Instead, I pulled out the drawer and placed it inside.

nine
band of hooligans

We still had the race to think about. Jacob showed up for practice the next morning, but he was quiet, and he barely spoke to me. I began a million conversations with him in my mind, but none of them sounded right. I kept wishing I had accepted that stuffed turtle and had not been such a brat at Coney Island.

For the rest of the week, we trained hard, pushing ourselves a little further each day. When I came home in the afternoons, my muscles ached. Ma ran the bath for me every night after dinner, sprinkling in a cup of Epsom salts, and then I soaked.

One day, after our five-mile run, I sat down on a shady

bench in the schoolyard, kicked off my sneakers, and looked around for Jacob. Annette was gabbing with someone by the water fountain, and Andy came and parked himself next to me. By that time, I'd gotten over my jitters and my wildly thumping heart at the sight of Andy.

"Where's Jacob?" he asked, scanning the field.

"I don't know. I was wondering the same thing."

Andy craned his neck and let his periscope eye search for Jacob. He kept talking. "He's been acting real moody since that fight with Douglas."

"Yeah, I know."

"Hey," he said, snapping his neck back into place, "why don't we do something together today to try and cheer him up? It's hot as the blazes. We could go to the pool."

"That sounds good."

Andy spotted Jacob in the distance. "Hey, pal!" he yelled. "We're going swimming!"

Annette and I went home to eat lunch and get our bathing suits on. The plan was to meet Andy at his house and then call for Jacob. Somewhere along the way, Roy managed to weasel into our plans. He whined and carried on. "Jacob's my friend, too!"

I swore, that kid was my cross to bear in life.

Andy's house was so noisy the windows rattled and the floors shook. His three younger brothers ran around the house playing war. One of them held a toy gun to my stomach. "It's curtains for you, you sneaky Jap! Pow! Pow! Pow!"

"Stop that, Jeff," his mother scolded, but he didn't listen to her.

Andy came out of the kitchen and smacked Jeff's rear end. Andy was the man of the house; a blue star in the window reminded everyone of that. His mother looked tired, like she was carrying lead weights on her shoulders.

"Oh, Andy," she said, "I forgot to tell you, there's a letter from your father on the dining room table."

Andy ran into the dining room, tore open the letter, and called out to us, "Hey, can you guys wait a second? I just want to read this."

"Sure," I said. Andy's mother tried to make small talk with us, but her band of hooligans kept interrupting us with shrieks and howls. Roy tried to join in with them, but I held him by the back of his shirt. As we left Andy's house, Jeff threw dirt-ball hand grenades at our backs and yelled, "Take that, you stinkin' Nazis!"

"Just you wait till I get home!" Andy said, waving his fist. "You better behave for Ma or I'll beat your behind."

We walked over to Jacob's house; it was the prettiest house on the street. Marigolds grew in window boxes, the porch was freshly painted, and the teeny garden was perfectly manicured. There was a blue star hanging in one of the windows; it was for his brother, Peter.

A knot grew in my stomach as we rang Jacob's bell. I'd never met Mr. Jacobsen. He didn't attend church with Jacob's mother, so I didn't even know what he looked like. I wondered if he was home. I hoped he was out on his fishing boat.

The door opened. "Well, well, who do we have here?" A cheerful man, quite a bit older than Pa, and smelling of freshly washed sheets, stepped out. He smiled and his face wrinkled. "Two lovely girls come to call on me? Come in, come in."

We walked into a fancy living room. "Mr. Jacobsen," Andy said, "this is Judy and Annette. They're running with us in the big race at Fort Hamilton."

Roy was waiting to be acknowledged. He stretched out his neck and said, "I'm Roy."

"So you are," said Mr. Jacobsen. "You're Judy's brother, aren't you?"

"Yep."

"I know your parents," he said. "Hulda and Sig—nice people." Mr. Jacobsen walked to the stairs and called, "Jacob. Some friends here to see you. Two of them are girls." He winked at me and Annette.

"Okay, Pa," we heard Jacob say. "I'll be there in a minute."

"So, Mr. Jacobsen," Andy said, "how long you home for?"

"Oh, three days, maybe four." He had a Norwegian singsong voice just like Pa's. "I was out digging clams for ten days. Made good money, but my knees are shot." He rubbed his knees and grimaced.

Jacob came down the stairs and waved to us. Then he saw Roy. "Hey, Roy, how ya doin'? Are you going swimming with us today?"

"Yep!" Roy smiled, crossed his arms over his chest, and gave me a smug look.

"I just need to grab something to eat," Jacob said. "I'll be right back." He headed for the kitchen.

Mr. Jacobsen sat down in an easy chair and motioned for us to join him. Andy carried the conversation, so I studied Mr. Jacobsen carefully. There were deep furrows around his light gray eyes, and his skin looked like tanned leather. His hands were strong and weather-beaten. His mouth had the same mischievous curve as Jacob's, and out of it came words filled with warmth and laughter.

I looked around the room. It was cozy and nicely decorated. There were small wood carvings all over the place, and each piece had something to do with the sea: fishermen, fishing boats, lobsters, dolphins, and whales. Roy noticed them too. "Mr. Jacobsen," he said, pointing around the room, "did you make all these?"

"Yes, I did. Go ahead, you can touch them if you like."

"Wow!" Roy said, breathing deeply and sliding his hand across one of the fishing boats. Roy continued to be nosy. "Who is this a picture of?" He picked up a framed photo of four people—two men in sailor uniforms with their arms around two girls.

"Those are my daughters, Ingrid and Aslaug, and the two men are their husbands. That picture was taken the day their husbands went overseas." I noticed that his daughters were smiling in the picture. I wondered if they went home and cried after that.

"Who's this?" Roy asked, holding up another picture. I was beginning to think Roy was making a nuisance of himself, but Mr. Jacobsen didn't seem to mind.

"That's my son Peter," he said. "He's chief engineer on his ship in the Pacific." Mr. Jacobsen looked very proud.

Jacob walked out of the kitchen, still chewing his food. Mr. Jacobsen stood up, reached into his pocket, and held out a few dollars. "Jacob," he said, "I want you to take these two beautiful girls and this very well-behaved little gentleman out for ice cream after you swim."

Jacob swallowed and looked at the money. "Thanks, Pa, but that's too much," he said in a stiff voice.

"Oh, nonsense." Mr. Jacobsen laughed. He took Jacob's hand and placed the bills into it.

"Thank you, Mr. Jacobsen," I said, trying to cover the awkwardness.

"My pleasure. And I suppose you can treat this fella too," he said as he tousled Andy's hair. "Looks like I have to put my scissors to your head soon, Andy."

"No thanks, Mr. Jacobsen. I'm already missing one eye—don't want to lose no ear."

"Ha! Go on. Have fun," Mr. Jacobsen said as he waved us out the door.

ten

no blood

I couldn't make heads or tails of Mr. Jacobsen.

Pa was no drinking man, but I remembered when he brought home a bottle of liquor one year around the holidays. It had been a gift from his first mate on the tugboat. Before he had even got a whiff of the stuff, Ma was pouring it down the kitchen sink, ranting and raving about it being the devil's drink. "There's only two kinds of Norwegians," she had hollered, "good ones and drinking ones, and there *certainly* won't be any drinking Norwegians in my house!" I grew up believing that any Norwegian who drank was in cahoots with the devil himself; hence, the dilemma of Mr. Jacobsen. He seemed like a pretty nice man.

The day Pa brought home that liquor, after Ma had had her fill of screaming at him, she cried until her eyes swelled like two Ping-Pong balls. Pa didn't get angry; he just held her and rocked her gently in his arms. He never brought home another bottle after that, that's for sure. I didn't know it then, but Ma was remembering all the bad things that had happened to her in Norway. I figured my real father must have been pretty awful to make Ma cry like that. When I looked in the mirror, I wondered if I looked anything like him. If I did, my face must have brought a heap of sorrow to Ma.

At the pool that day, Annette did some cockamamie jump off the diving board and twisted her ankle. She sat on the edge of the pool, mad as a wet hornet. It must have hurt real bad, because she said some hells and damns through her teeth. I was kind of surprised. On top of the no-dancing rule, Norwegian Lutherans were not allowed to curse. Annette pounded the pavement with her fist.

"Gosh, don't break your hand, too," Jacob said.

"Shut up! Go away!"

"What about the race?" I said.

That made her really sore, and she nearly chomped my head off. "What do you mean? I'll be fine!" But she wasn't. Andy and Jacob took turns carrying her, piggyback, all the way home. They plopped her on my stoop, and I went inside for some ice. I hacked away at the block in the icebox, got a few chunks, and wrapped them in an old rag. When I came out, Harold was there, talking to the three of them.

"Hey, Judy," Harold said, sounding all put out, "how come you didn't tell me about the race?"

I bent down and wrapped the ice around Annette's ankle. "I don't know, Harold. Do I have to tell you everything?"

"Well, it's a pretty big deal," he said. "A race at Fort Hamilton."

Jacob piped up. "You know, you're a fast runner, Harold. I've seen you at school."

"Yeah," Harold said. "I'm not bad."

I looked at Jacob. "So, what are you trying to say?"

"Well, I don't think Annette can run on that ankle. Maybe Harold can take her place."

I looked at Annette. Her mouth was hanging open. Andy sat down next to her and peeked under the rag that held the ice. "It's real swollen," he said.

Annette screwed up her face, then kicked a stone with her good foot. "Fine," she said, glaring at Harold. "You wanna run for me?"

"Yeah, I could do that."

"Well, you better not mess it up. We've been working hard."

Andy put his arm around Annette and patted her back. "Hey," he said, "you sit here and rest. Keep that ice on. Me and Jacob are gonna go down and buy you a bag of candy. Maybe that'll cheer you up a little. What kind do you like?"

Annette moped a little longer; then she said, "Red licorice sounds good." Andy nodded, and he and Jacob headed for the candy store.

When they reached the corner, Annette looked at Harold and smirked. "So, what's the deal, Harold?" she said.

"All of a sudden you're friendly with Jacob? I thought you didn't like him."

"Yeah, well, he's all right," Harold said. "I figure anyone who stands up to O'Reilly has to be worth something. He stood up to me, too, that day at the pool when I dunked Judy. The kid's got a lot of guts."

Annette rolled her eyes at me and shook her head. We both laughed. And when the boys came back with the licorice, she shared it with all of us.

It turned out Harold was almost as fast as Annette, and pretty soon the four of us became a team. Annette's father was a carpenter, so he made her a pair of crutches with some leftover wood from one of his jobs. She and Olaf became our cheering squad. In the long run, Annette was a pretty good sport about it.

When we weren't running, Harold and Jacob spent their time trying to outdo each other and impress me. They arm wrestled, thumb wrestled, compared biceps, and had contests to see who could jump the highest over a johnny pump. Andy scratched his head at them, but I saw how he fussed over Annette's ankle, sliding his hand over it and checking the swelling every day. I saw them make googly eyes at each other, and I was glad I'd gotten over my crush on Andy.

I felt bad for Olaf, though; he'd been in love with Annette since kindergarten. One morning, before practice, he came to my door. I was still in my pajamas. "What is it, Olaf?" I said, poking my head out. "It's kind of early; is something wrong?"

He shuffled his feet around and stuffed his hands in his pockets. "I just want to know if Annette likes Andy."

"Oh." I thought for a minute. How could I say this without hurting his feelings? "I don't know, Olaf. She hasn't said anything to me yet, but honestly, yeah, I think she does."

"So, you don't think I have a chance with her. I should give up."

"Well . . . I guess that's up to you, but it doesn't look too good."

He sighed deeply, then hung his head. "All right, I just thought I'd ask. I'll see you later, Judy." I watched him shuffle away.

Later that afternoon, in the middle of practice, I was slurping water from the fountain and Andy walked over to me. He had a big grin on his face. "Jacob's sweet on you, he said."

I nearly choked. "What did you say?"

"Jacob's sweet on you."

"Well, that's news to me." But it wasn't. I'd known all along. It was just strange to hear out loud.

I took another drink and watched Andy walk back to the track. My stomach was flopping around and I didn't feel much like running anymore. I wanted to sit on a bench and figure out what was happening with all my friends. And with me, too. Everything was changing. But then I heard Andy calling me. "Come on, Judy! We're not finished yet! Four more laps!"

After practice, I told Annette about Olaf's visit to my house that morning. She laughed out loud. "Harold asked me the same thing today," she said, "about you and Jacob."

"He did? You're kidding? What did you say?"

"I told him to stop being such a ninny. If he wants to know how you feel about Jacob, he should ask you himself."

"You said that? Oh my gosh, Annette." I laughed, picturing what Harold's face must have looked like. "What are we going to do with the two of them?" I asked.

"Nothing," Annette said. "Ignore them."

And so, for lack of a better plan, I agreed.

That week, as we continued to train for the race, Douglas O'Reilly and his gang went on to bigger and better things. We heard rumors that they were starting trouble with some boys on Fifth Avenue, so we didn't see them around. All of us were relieved, and as the days went by, Jacob seemed more relaxed. He smiled and joked around with us. Sometimes I caught him staring at me, and when I did, I looked away. But I wondered what he was thinking.

Pa came home a couple of days before the race and tried to squeeze me and give me a kiss hello. Ma had asked me to greet him nicely this time and to tell him about the race, but I couldn't do it. "Pa! Remember?" I said. "I'm thirteen years old!" Deep inside, I wanted to hold him tight and laugh while he twirled me around, the way he used to do when I was little. Instead, I watched him do it to Roy.

Finally, the day of the race arrived. The crowd was festive, waving banners and cheering us on. Pa was perched on the bleachers with Ma, Roy, and Harold's parents; Annette and Olaf were sitting at the finish line; and Andy's mother chased her three boys around the field. Jacob's folks were nowhere in sight. Amid the crowd, I saw Douglas and four of his tagalongs, but I didn't tell Jacob.

We took our starting positions on the track. I was first leg, and when the gun went off, my feet flew. I could barely feel them. I took the lead and handed the baton off to Harold. We were tied for second when Jacob took over, and then Andy sprang into first on the final leg of the race. He crossed the finish line with two fists in the air.

The crowd went wild with excitement, and we flung our arms around each other in victory. I could feel our bodies, warm and soaked with sweat, but it felt good and natural. We ran to Annette and Olaf and wrapped our arms around them, too. I could hear Pa's voice rising above the crowd: "That's my girl! That's my girl!" At first I laughed, but then those words made me feel strange inside.

The judges handed us a big trophy, and we decided to celebrate at the ice cream parlor. Jacob held the trophy over his head as we walked toward the avenue. I don't think any of us had ever felt happier in all our lives. Then we saw Douglas and his gang waiting for us at the corner.

"So, Jacobsen!" he said. "You think you're pretty hot stuff now with that stupid trophy?"

My heart thumped in my throat. Jacob tucked the trophy under his arm, and Andy motioned for us to keep walking. Douglas and his gang spread out in front of us.

"Give it up, already, Douglas!" Harold yelled.

As we passed them, one of the gang shoved Andy and said, "Hey, it's the one-eyed freak who runs with the girls. Are you gonna go play hopscotch with them now?"

Jacob lunged at him, but Andy held Jacob back. Andy looked at the kid and said, "I wouldn't waste my time on scum like you."

"Hey, Jacobsen," Douglas said. "Didn't see your father at the race today. He must have one *nasty* hangover. He sure made my father rich last night. Blew all his money buying rounds for his squarehead buddies. He was so drunk, your mother had to drag him home again." Douglas and his gang laughed and snorted.

Andy held Jacob tight. "Don't let him get to you, Jacob. He ain't worth it."

We made it past Douglas without any blood. Jacob stuffed his hands in his pockets and walked ahead of us, but Andy and Harold caught up to him. Andy looped his arm around Jacob's shoulder, and Harold talked about how he was gonna get back at those creeps. By the time we reached the ice cream parlor, Jacob seemed to have shaken it off.

We ordered French fries, egg creams, and ice cream sundaes; then we played stickball together for the rest of the afternoon. After that, Andy went home to help his mother with chores, and Jacob came to our house to help Roy with his pinewood derby car. They were going to work on it in the basement, and before they headed downstairs, Ma invited Jacob to stay for dinner.

Ma cooked, and Pa relaxed on the sofa, listening to the radio. The news came on with Gabriel Heattor announcing,

"One million men are marching, and they all use Kreml." I thought that was pretty silly. I didn't think soldiers would care too much about hair tonic with all those bombs and bullets flying around.

"Judy," Pa said, patting the spot next to him. "Will you come and sit with me?" I hesitated at first, then walked over and lowered myself to the sofa. He wrapped his big bear arms around me.

"Pa! You're suffocating me!" He still had the smell of diesel fuel from the tugboat on his clothes, and it mixed with his aftershave. "And you stink!" I pushed him away, but he held on to my hand.

"Tomorrow we leave for the Catskills," he said. "Are you excited?"

It was the first of August, and we'd be leaving to spend a full month in the Catskill Mountains. We went every summer, and normally I couldn't wait for it to come. Now I wasn't so sure.

My hand started to sweat, so I pulled it away. "It'll be fun, Pa. But I'm gonna miss my friends."

"Oh," he said, "a month goes by so fast. They'll be right here when you get back. Besides, you'll have Audrey."

"Yeah, I guess so," I said, thinking about my friend Audrey, who lived up in the Catskills. I sighed, leaned back on the sofa, and thought about our trip. Pa would be with us for the first two weeks, and that made me nervous. The year before, he took me into town every morning and let me drive along some country roads. (We didn't mention this to Ma, of course.) Then, in the afternoons, we swam across the lake together. I remembered having a lot of fun, but now part of me was anxious about spending this time alone with him.

"I still can't believe the way you ran in that race," Pa said, smiling. "I'm so proud of you. I knew you were fast, but I didn't know you could run like the wind."

I looked into his eyes, but all I could feel was the ache inside. No race, no trophy, no vacation, no number of friends could take it away. My eyes started to sting, so I closed them and lay down on the sofa. My body felt tired from the day. As Pa listened to the radio, I listened to the rhythm of his breathing and it lulled me to sleep. I dreamed of the Catskill Mountains and the bright blue sky.

eleven

fish balls and creamed cabbage

I awoke to loud voices mixed with the aroma of fish balls and creamed cabbage. Ma was fretting in the kitchen, the way she did when she burned something. Pots and pans were banging, and Pa's voice was deep and serious. I wiped the drool from the side of my mouth, and the next thing I knew, a tremendous weight landed right on my chest. It was Roy. He looked like a lunatic, and he was screaming something into my face.

"Get off of me!" I said, pushing him to the floor.

"Judy, Jacob's missing! We have to find him!"

"Come on, Roy. Do you really think Jacob would take

off before we ate? He's probably in the bathroom combing his hair or something."

"We already ate," he said.

"You mean . . . without me?" I became aware of the emptiness in my stomach. I sat up and rubbed my eyes.

Pa walked into the room. "Judy, we need your help. Jacob left for home over an hour ago. His mother just called and said he's not there yet. Do you have any idea where he could be?"

I felt like saying, "Why did everyone eat without me?" but I figured that wouldn't go over too well. My head felt scrambled. "How about Andy's house, or Harold's? Did anyone check there?"

"Mrs. Jacobsen called Andy and all of Jacob's friends. He's nowhere," Pa said.

Ma came into the living room with a plate of food for me. Beads of sweat covered her forehead. "Judy needs to eat something before she can think."

Ma, Pa, and Roy stared at me while I chewed my fish ball. I thought about Douglas and his gang, and then I put down my fork. "Pa, I think Jacob may be in trouble. We better go look for him. He could be hurt."

As Pa and I scouted the neighborhood, I told him about our run-in with Douglas after the race. Pa shook his head and frowned. When we got to the elementary school, I saw two figures in the playground. The smaller figure was sitting at the bottom of a slide; the larger one was kneeling next to him. "Pa, look! There's Jacob with his father."

I ran over to them, but when I got close, I wanted to

disappear. Jacob's face was swollen and covered with dried blood. His father had one hand stretched out to him and one hand covering his own face. I took a step back, but Mr. Jacobsen glanced up at me and said, "No, Judy, please don't go. Maybe he'll talk to you. He won't say a word to me."

Pa came over, put his arm around Mr. Jacobsen, and whispered something in his ear. He helped him to his feet, and then the two of them began walking home. I was left alone with Jacob.

"Pa!" I called after him. He turned around and looked at me, but he just nodded and continued on. I knelt down next to Jacob and said, "It was Douglas, wasn't it?"

"Yeah. He and his friends jumped me. He said next time they'd put me in the hospital." Jacob looked at me, and through the swollen slits of his eyes, I could see an angry blue.

"Why don't you come to our house? Ma can clean you up."

"I can take care of myself," he said. "Please, just go away."

The words stung, but I knew he didn't mean it. I knew he wanted me to stay. He said it because he hurt inside, and I understood how he felt.

I wasn't sure what to do, so I parked myself on a bench and prayed for wisdom. Ma had taught me to do that. She was big on praying. Distant voices from the apartment buildings blew around the abandoned park, and an ambulance siren wailed near the hospital. I listened closely, hoping to hear God whisper to me in the wind. I waited, but nothing came. Ma told me that God answers our prayers in his time, and in all different ways.

I stood up and walked over to Jacob. As I knelt down next to him, a strange sensation came over me. It was like I could feel all his anger and shame. It was awful. I wondered if it had something to do with my prayer. I held out my hand to him; he took it, and we started walking home.

That night I had a really bad dream. I woke up screaming, and Ma came running into my bedroom.

"Judy," she said, wrapping her arms around me. "It's just a dream."

I held on to Ma. I was breathing hard, and my nightgown was damp with sweat. In my dream, the faceless man with dark hair was chasing me through the streets of the city, and I couldn't find my way home.

"Everything's okay," Ma whispered. "Do you want to tell me your dream? Will that help?"

"No, Ma. I'm all right."

"Are you sure?"

"I'm sure. I'll be fine. I'm sorry I woke you."

"Oh, that's okay." She took my hand, and even in the dim light, I could see how worried she looked. "Now, try to think of something good before you sleep," she said. "Think of the mountains—we'll be there tomorrow." Ma kissed my cheek and I breathed in her smell. It seemed like lately we'd grown so distant, and I wondered if it was just me who had pulled away, or if it was both of us. I was so mixed up I couldn't tell.

twelve

shrimp salad sandwiches and chocolate milk

Ma was frantic the next morning, trying to do a million things at once. Cooking, cleaning, packing, and fussing, she always got a little nutty the day we left for the Catskills. I woke up late and stumbled into the kitchen, looking for coffee. Ma was emptying out the icebox, and bacon and eggs were sizzling in the pan.

She hurried to the stove and flipped the eggs. "Good morning, Judy." Then she poured me a cup of coffee, popped her head out the back door, and called Pa in for breakfast. He was in the garage, working on the car. It was actually an old jalopy that had only one purpose in life: to get us to and from the Catskills in one piece. Ma had taken it in to the gas station each week to get our three-gallon ration, and now it was full to the brim.

Pa walked inside, covered with grease. He started saying something to Ma in Norwegian, but she interrupted. "Pa, *snakke engelsk*—talk English." Ma was real particular about that. The teachers in school told her that English should be the only language spoken around the children. We all needed to assimilate.

"Listen, Ma," he said, "when this war is finally over, I'm going to buy you the shiniest, fanciest, brand-newest car you've ever seen."

Ma shook her head and said, "Now, wash those filthy hands and come to the table." Pa kept trying to hug her with his greasy hands, but Ma wasn't in a playful mood. She shooed him away. "*Uff da!* Wash those hands!"

Roy joined us, and as we sat down to eat, Ma cleared her throat and made an announcement. "Jacob will be coming with us."

I dropped my fork. "What?" I thought maybe I hadn't heard right. I looked at Pa, but he kept right on eating.

Roy was grinning so hard, I thought his ears were gonna start flapping. "Wow, Ma, that's great! This is gonna be the best summer yet!"

"We don't have enough room," I said.

"We'll make room," Ma said, looking down at her plate. "I spoke with Mrs. Jacobsen this morning and everything's settled."

"Where, may I ask, is he going to sleep?" I said.

No one answered. That did it. He was going to take my

room—I knew it. I got up from the table, ran upstairs, and flung myself onto my bed.

This was too much. Now, on top of everything else, we had to cart Jacob along with us. Our bungalow in the Catskills was so tiny the four of us barely fit. What if I had another one of my dreams while we were up there? What if I woke up screaming again? Jacob would be sure to hear. What if he found out my secret? I was angry at Ma. Why did she have to do this? I pounded my fist into the pillow.

There were things I didn't want to share with Jacob. Maybe I was being selfish, but our summer vacation was special to me. It was for *our* family, and Jacob would be an intruder.

First, on the drive up there was lunch at the Red Apple, where Pa would buy us shrimp salad sandwiches and chocolate milk. There were games of croquet we'd play in back of our bungalow, and stacks of comic books we'd read together when we got bored. There were our daily swims at the lake, and our trips into town.

There were secret places that only I knew about. Beautiful spots in the woods where I'd bring my pencils and my paintbrushes and spend the day translating it all onto paper. Having Jacob there would be nothing but a nuisance, like a mosquito buzzing in my ear or a blister on the back of my heel.

Then I thought about my friend Audrey and how we'd meet at the lake, go swimming, and eat Popsicles at the covered stand. I didn't want to share her, either.

Pa came up to my room. "Listen, Judy," he said, "I

know this is hard for you, but please try to understand. Jacob's in trouble, and his mother's afraid. She doesn't know what to do. If we take him out of the city for a while, by the time he gets back, those boys will have cooled down—maybe even forgotten the whole thing. You can see that, can't you?"

I stared down at my mattress. I wanted to scream, "What about me? Don't I count for anything?"

"Why don't you come downstairs," Pa said. "You didn't finish your breakfast."

"I'm not hungry."

He stood there for a minute. "All right. Well, do you need help packing? Maybe Ma should come up a little later and help you."

"No," I said, irritated that he asked me this. "I'm not a little kid. I can do it myself."

Pa sighed, shook his head, and went downstairs. After a while, I got up from my bed and pulled a suitcase from my closet. I opened the top drawer of my dresser, scooped out a stack of underwear, and placed it in one corner of the suitcase. I noticed that the pair on top was dingy and torn at the seam. I can't take those with me, I thought. What if Jacob sees them? I balled them up and shoved them back into my drawer. Then I pulled out two bras (the training kind with triple-A cups) and felt sick at the thought of Jacob seeing them on the clothesline in back of our bungalow. I got angry all over again. I pulled out the rest of my drawers, dumped all my clothes into the suitcase, zipped it up, and told myself I didn't care.

I sat there for a while, feeling completely miserable.

Then I realized I had forgotten the most important thing. I went back to my closet and got out the special case that Pa had bought me last year for my art supplies. I took it to my desk and opened it carefully. I put back the paints and brushes I'd been using recently, then closed it up. I carried it downstairs, along with my suitcase, and placed them both by the front door. Then I went into the kitchen and helped Ma with the rest of the cleaning and packing. The two of us barely spoke. Pretty soon we were ready to go.

Pa loaded up the car while Roy and I said good-bye to our friends. I gave Annette a big hug and told her what had happened. "So he's coming with us," I said.

"Wow." She glanced at Harold and Olaf, who were making their way toward us. "You better not say anything to Harold right now; he's jealous enough already. I'll tell him later."

Roy put his arm around Pauley, who was sitting on his stoop crying; Roy was his only friend on the block. I gave Harold and Olaf quick hugs and then we hopped into the car and headed over to Fifty-second Street. On the way, Ma warned Roy to stay in the car when we picked up Jacob, and not to say too much.

When we pulled up to the house, Jacob was sitting outside with Andy, and it was hard to read the expression on his face because it was so swollen and black and blue. Ma gasped when she saw him, clicked her tongue a few times, and looked at me. I looked away.

Ma got out and spoke with Mrs. Jacobsen while I thumped my fingers against the car door. Roy squirmed on the seat next to me. They talked quietly in Norwegian, which meant they didn't want us to hear what they were saying. Then Mrs. Jacobsen handed Ma an envelope with cash in it, which Ma objected to, so Mrs. Jacobsen stuffed it into Ma's purse. Ma sighed, and they hugged each other good-bye.

Pa got out and helped Mr. Jacobsen load a suitcase into our trunk. Then Mr. Jacobsen walked over to Jacob and held out his hand, but Jacob quickly turned away; he climbed into the backseat of our car next to Roy. A second later, Andy stuck his head in. "You guys take care of him, all right?"

"Sure," I said.

"Take it easy, Jacob," Andy said, patting him on the shoulder.

Mrs. Jacobsen came over; she bent down and kissed Jacob on the cheek, smoothing his hair back. "Bye, Ma," he said. She whispered something in his ear and he nodded; then she closed the car door. After Ma and Pa said their last good-byes, we took off. I was glad that Roy was sitting between me and Jacob. I didn't want to talk to Jacob.

Roy jabbered nonstop while I gazed out the window and said good-bye to the city. I breathed in all the city smells as we traveled uptown. I watched the neighborhoods change from good to bad to slummy, and back to good again; houses to brownstones to crummy-looking apartments to penthouses. As we drove through Harlem, I saw some kids running through the water gushing from an open johnny pump.

It was hard to keep cool on those steamy city streets. *Goodbye, city*.

When we got on Route 17, I knew it wouldn't be long before we reached the Red Apple. My stomach was empty and growling, and I remembered the bacon and eggs I'd left on my plate that morning. I cleared my throat and said, "We'll be at the Red Apple soon."

Pa turned around and said, "She talks!"

The Red Apple was one of those cafeteria-type places where you got on line, took a tray, and picked out what you wanted. When we got there, Jacob parked himself at a table and stared at the floor. Ma, Pa, and Roy headed over to the line, but I stepped up to Jacob and folded my arms across my chest. "They don't serve you here," I said. "You have to get your own food."

He glanced up at me. "I'm not hungry."

I tapped my foot for a while; then pulled out a chair, making a loud screech, and sat down. I saw Pa squinting across the room, watching the two of us. I was really irritated, but when I looked at Jacob's face, all bashed up and black and blue, I remembered everything from the night before, and suddenly I felt very ashamed. I didn't say anything for a while; then I took a deep breath. "Listen, Jacob, I'm sorry. I've been pretty awful. Why don't we go over and get something to eat? They have really good shrimp salad sandwiches and chocolate milk. Come on, I'll show you."

Slowly, Jacob got out of his chair, and I led him to the

line. I filled up his tray with the best food and we ate together at our own table. I told him about our little bungalow and about Mrs. Breuger, the strange old lady across the road who was always spying on us. I told him about the lake, the diving board, and the slippery, floating log we would try to walk across. I told him about the families we would meet at the lake, and what incredible hillbillies they were. Jacob listened and didn't say much, but I could tell his heart was growing a little lighter now that he had a friend.

thirteen

a resting place

"Krumville, here we come!" Pa said as we passed the sign that read, KRUMVILLE—2 MILES.

Jacob looked at me and mouthed, "Krumville?"

I nodded and whispered, "It's named after Mr. and Mrs. Krum."

"Oh."

It was funny how every year we came back the bungalow seemed to shrink. "It looks smaller," Roy said when we got there.

"No, it's the same," Pa said. "You just got bigger."

Our little house, as I called it, actually belonged to Mrs. Breuger. We rented it from her. As soon as we pulled up, she poked her head out her front door and hobbled over to us. Mrs. Breuger looked ancient, maybe more than a hundred years old. Her face was shriveled like a raisin, and she was missing a lot of teeth. For some reason her head shook like crazy. One time Roy asked Ma whether the bungalow would belong to us if Mrs. Breuger dropped dead. Ma laughed and said Mrs. Breuger was as strong as an ox and as stubborn as a mule, and would probably outlive us all. I found that hard to believe.

Mrs. Breuger held out a withered hand with a key dangling on the end of it, bobbed her head around a bit, and said, "Here's the key. I'll get the cats for you." Then she hobbled back across the road. Mrs. Breuger had a million cats. She loaned us a few every summer to catch the mice that were living in our bungalow. It was kind of disgusting, because during our first week there, we'd find dead mice on the floor every morning. Pa scooped them up into a bucket, but it was my job to bury them out in the woods. When I buried the mice, Roy came with me and scattered wildflowers over their graves.

When we arrived, Ma began her cleaning frenzy and shooed us all out of the house. Pa headed for the hammock, and Roy ran off to visit Billy, his friend who lived up the road. My only friend, Audrey, didn't live within walking distance. I would see her when we drove to the lake.

Jacob and I decided to take a walk. He'd never been out of the city before, and I laughed while he looked with amazement at all the trees and flowers. "It smells so good here," he said, taking a deep breath. We climbed a hill and picked a bunch of tiger lilies for Ma; then we sat in the grass and enjoyed the breeze. "It's nice and cool, too," he said, "much cooler than the city."

I smiled. "We're in the mountains; that's why."

When we returned, the house smelled like ammonia and everything was shiny and clean. Ma really liked the flowers. She placed them in a vase and set it on the kitchen table. "I saw you brought your art supplies, Judy," she said. "I'm glad. I was hoping you'd continue your painting this summer."

I tensed up when Ma said this in front of Jacob. My artwork was private in a way, and I had a hard time talking about it. I was thrilled last year, though, when my art teacher said I had talent. She'd hung my work on display, and all my friends took notice; even Annette, who only cared about sports, was impressed. But still, I didn't say much about it.

"Yes," I said quietly. "I'm going to work on some landscapes."

"Do you think I could watch you paint sometime?" Jacob said. "I'd like to see how you do it."

"Oh, I don't know." This made me uneasy, but part of me liked that Jacob was interested. "I guess so, if you want."

"Pa was talking about having you start private lessons with Mrs. Marshall this fall," Ma said.

I almost fell over when I heard this. I always thought it would be wonderful to take art lessons, but I never thought it was possible. Mrs. Marshall charged four dollars an hour. "But, Ma," I said, "they're expensive."

Ma nodded. "They are expensive, but Pa says we can afford it."

I stood there for a while, and I didn't know what to say. I wondered if Ma and Pa were doing this to make up for things because they felt bad for me. I'm not sure why, but it made me angry. Did they think I needed their sympathy? "I don't want art lessons," I said.

Ma looked shocked at first, then hurt. I walked out of the kitchen and went outside to the porch. I was having trouble breathing. Jacob came out after me. "Judy," he said. "What's the matter?"

"Nothing," I said. "I don't want to talk about it."

"Did I say something wrong?"

"No, it's not you. I just want to be alone for a while."

Jacob stood there with a puzzled look on his face; then he went back into the house. I set off for another walk, and along the way I kept thinking about what it would be like to take those art lessons. I remembered walking into Mrs. Marshall's room when my eighth-grade class had gone for a tour of the high school. Covering the walls were paintings done by her private students. I imagined one of my paintings hanging up there, and the thought was so exciting it made me dizzy. What is wrong with me? I thought. Why couldn't I just accept Ma's offer?

When I got back, it was time to work out the sleeping arrangements. There were only two bedrooms in the house. The larger one had two double beds; Ma and Pa shared one, and Roy had the other. The smaller room, which had been mine in previous years, had a single bed. It would be Jacob's room this summer, and I would share a bed with Roy.

When Roy came back from Billy's house, I was tucking sheets onto the mattress. I remembered Roy's accident in the middle of the night last year; Ma said he'd caught a chill. I pointed my finger at Roy's nose and said, "You better not wet this here bed, mister."

Roy scowled. "I don't do that anymore."

I sure hoped not.

We unpacked the rest of our things and washed up for dinner. Pa barbecued hamburgers and Ma boiled corn on the cob. Mrs. Breuger came over with a big barrel of peaches from her tree, and Ma invited her to eat with us. We toasted marshmallows and stayed outside until the mosquitoes grew too thick.

That night, I lay awake in bed thinking. I couldn't do much else, because Roy was scratching mosquito bites in his sleep, and Pa was snoring like a freight train. I decided that Pa was right; Jacob did need to get out of the city, away from Douglas and all the trouble, and having him with us might not be so bad after all. I just wouldn't worry about things like ripped underwear or training bras on the clothesline. And now that we were in the Catskills, maybe my dreams would be good ones; already the fresh air was making me feel better. I wouldn't worry about Jacob learning my secret, either. It was locked away, safe inside me.

I wondered if Jacob was asleep, so I got up, peeked into his room, and heard the steady rhythm of his breathing. I was glad he'd found a resting place.

fourteen
puberty

Ma was frying bacon and eggs when I walked into the kitchen the next morning. "Judy, will you call everyone in for breakfast?" she asked.

"Sure, Ma." I opened the front door and found Jacob perched on the railing of our porch. He was in deep conversation with Mrs. Breuger. A tiny calico kitten was nestled in his lap. The kitten had patches of orange and white, and a big black spot covered its nose.

I never got that close to Mrs. Breuger. She smelled like mothballs, and besides her head rattling around, she whistled through what few teeth she had left. She really gave me the creeps. One time she toddled right up to me, looked at my feet, and told me I needed to trim my toenails. That's when I decided she was crazy and I needed to stay away from her.

"Jacob, Ma's got breakfast ready," I said from the door. I found Pa and Roy setting up for croquet in the back of the house and called them in for breakfast, too.

Ma liked to kiss us before we ate, and she gave the slobberiest kisses you could ever imagine. During the meal, I would use my napkin to wipe the slobber, pretending to wipe some food from my face. That morning, after we'd said grace, she got up and kissed Roy first. I was wondering if she was going to plant one on Jacob. She did. He didn't even wince; he looked up at her and smiled. When she came to me, she rubbed my cheek for a second. "Are you okay, Judy?"

"Yes, Ma," I said.

"Good," she said, and kissed me gently.

When Jacob finished eating, he helped Ma clear the dishes and he said, *"Takk for maten*—thank you for the food." Ma loved that.

After a few morning chores, we packed sandwiches, jumped into our jalopy, and headed for the lake. Roy and Jacob made plans to build a triple-decker dam in the sand, and I was looking forward to seeing Audrey. She and I had had a great time together the previous summer, and we'd written to each other during the school year. We were in the same grade, but Audrey was about six months older than me. She had already turned fourteen.

We parked our chairs and towels next to Ma's friend Boots, who was practically jumping up and down when she saw us. She went by "Boots" because it was her maiden name, but she seemed like the kind of lady who would wear red galoshes in the rain. Boots was from the city also, on vacation just like us, and found it hard to mix with the country folks. She usually had her two sons with her, but this year they had been drafted. Boots had lots of spunk, but she looked older and grayer than I had remembered. I wondered if it was because she missed her sons. Her husband, Tom, seemed especially quiet this year.

I looked around for Audrey and spotted her on the big wooden raft in the center of the lake. She was surrounded by a group of boys who were trying to tip the raft over. The lifeguard blew his whistle at them, but they ignored him. I ran to the dock and jumped in. The water was icy cold, so I swam hard and fast out to the raft. "Hey, Audrey!" I called.

"Judy, is it really you?"

"Yep," I said, hopping onto the raft.

"Boys, this is my friend Judy," she said.

Boys? She knew them? I wasn't expecting an introduction. They mumbled something in my direction and went back to rocking the raft back and forth.

Audrey had changed a lot in the past year. She had grown breasts and hips, and her legs were shapely. She looked like one big curve. I suddenly became very aware of my hairpin figure as I stood next to her. When she smiled, though, she was the same Audrey, and we gave each other a big hug. "Come on, let's get out of here," she said as she gracefully dove into the lake. I just lowered myself into the water. I still

84

had the drowning phobia, and it was especially strong around a bunch of rowdy boys.

After we swam for a while, we dried off and headed to the snack bar. We bought cherry Popsicles, and plopped down in the sand to eat them. "Who's that with Roy?" Audrey asked. Her lips were red from the Popsicle, and she looked like she was wearing lipstick.

"Jacob. He's staying with us this summer."

She took a closer look at him. "He's cute—*very* cute."

"Cute?" I said. "His face is all black and blue; how can you tell?"

"Oh, believe me, I can tell. He's living with you? Was he in a fight or something?" Audrey's eyes were like big saucers of cream.

"Yeah." I told her the story, omitting the part about Jacob's father being a drunk. That was too personal.

"Well," she said, "ain't you gonna introduce me?"

I shrugged. "If you like." I got a sick feeling in my stomach as we walked over to Jacob and Roy. I watched Audrey's hips sway back and forth as she combed her fingers through her hair.

"Hi, Jacob," she said before I could get any words out.

He looked up at her and then at me. "Hi," he said. Then he went back to building the dam.

I cleared my throat and managed to squeak out, "Jacob, this is my friend Audrey."

"Get lost," Roy said. "We're building a dam."

"Oh, can we help?" Audrey asked.

Jacob shrugged. "If you want. Is that okay with you, Roy?"

"Oh, all right, but you better do what we say," Roy said. "Jacob and I planned it all out." So that afternoon, we built a dam. I took orders from Roy, and no one else talked to me. I watched Audrey make saucer eyes at Jacob, and I endured her giggly conversation. I hated to admit it, but I was jealous; it was the worst feeling in the world. Boots was watching us the whole time. She kept clearing her throat and eyeballing Audrey from a distance. Boots was a sharp lady.

I didn't talk to Jacob for the rest of the day. After dinner he spent time with Mrs. Breuger and the black-nosed kitten, and I just moped around. That night, when Pa and Ma came into the bedroom, I pretended to be asleep. I heard them talking about my moodiness. "It's just puberty," Ma said. With her Norwegian accent it sounded like "pooberty."

I wanted to scream.

fifteen

little honey

The next morning I wanted to be alone, so I got dressed and stepped outside. The air felt cool and crisp, but the sun warmed my face and shoulders. I breathed in the honeysuckle that grew wild along the fence. "Ma, I'm going for a walk," I called.

A minute later, the screen door flew open and Jacob barreled out after me. "Hey, Judy, wait up! Where ya goin'?" I plowed ahead and didn't answer him. "Why are you so mad at me?" he asked, trailing by my side.

I looked straight ahead and walked faster. "I'm not mad at you," I said.

"So why are you acting like this?"

"I'm not acting any particular way." We hiked about a mile in silence. Then I said, "Did you have a good time at the lake yesterday?"

"Yeah."

"Did you have a *lovely* time with Audrey?"

"No. Is that what you're mad about?"

"I'm not mad—remember?"

Jacob scrunched his eyebrows together and said, "If you want my honest opinion, I think Audrey's got nothing but hot air between her ears, and her mouth never stops yapping. And . . . she's not nearly as pretty as you."

"Shut up," I said. We tramped about another mile. I didn't want to admit it, but I was glad Jacob had said what he had. On the road ahead, I saw the path that led to my favorite and most secret spot. "Jacob," I said. "Come on, there's something I want to show you." We hopped a fence where some cows were grazing, and we scrambled through the woods until we came to a clearing.

The spot was just as I remembered it: a field, covered in flowers, with a pond in the middle, chock-full of frogs croaking and hopping. There must have been a million butterflies floating around. An enormous oak tree shaded the clearing, and suspended from one of its branches was a tire swing. Next to the pond was a big old bathtub filled with rainwater. We walked to the pond; I reached down and cupped my hands around a frog and put him in the bathtub for a swim. "Do you like it?" I asked Jacob.

"It's amazing."

We caught ten frogs and gave them each a swim in the

bathtub. After that, we took turns pushing and spinning each other on the tire swing; then we picked a bunch of flowers. Jacob was going to press some in a book and take them back to the city. After a while, we sat down in the grass to rest. "Doesn't this place belong to someone?" Jacob asked. "I mean, what if they caught us here?"

"I don't know," I said. "I always thought it belonged to me." I lay down, and the grass felt cool on my back.

"Well," Jacob said, "I guess now it belongs to *us*." He turned to me and smiled, and this time I didn't look away.

It felt good to be there with him; all the sad things kind of melted away. I told Jacob I'd bring my sketchbook and watercolors the next time we came to that spot. He told me again that he'd like to watch me paint, maybe even learn a few things if he could. When we started for home, he said, "Thanks for not asking a bunch of questions. You know, about my father and all."

It made me nervous when he said that. "Well," I said, "I just didn't think you'd want to talk about it."

Jacob looked at the ground. "I've never really talked to anyone about it. Well, except for Andy, and there are some things I haven't told him." He raised his head and squinted into the distance. "I don't want you to think my father's a bad person. I mean, he'd never hurt me, or my mother, or anyone."

"I never thought that," I said, although that was not exactly true. Before I met Jacob's father, I thought he was a bad man.

"My mother," Jacob went on, "she's begged him to stop

drinking, but he goes to the bars anyway, after his fishing trips. Sometimes she goes out in the middle of the night to bring him home. I told her not to do it, but she said he might wind up in the gutter." Jacob kicked a stone across the road. "It makes me sick when I see him like that."

I didn't know what to say. My legs started to feel heavy, like I could barely put one foot in front of the other.

Jacob turned to me, then stopped. "You know, one night I followed my mother to the bar and spied from a window. Those stupid, drunk friends of his laughed at her, they said some nasty things, but she just took him home and put him to bed. You know, it's terrible, but sometimes I feel angry at her, too." He shook his head. "Isn't that stupid? Like it's her fault or something."

When Jacob said this, it felt like something hit me in the chest. I thought about the way I'd been treating Ma, like it was her fault everything had happened; and how I'd been treating Pa, like it was his fault that I wasn't his real daughter.

We started walking again, and we were both quiet. After a while, Jacob said, "My father came home drunk on Christmas Eve last year. Can you imagine? It ruined our whole Christmas."

"That's awful," I said.

I remembered our last Christmas. We were at Tante Anna and Uncle John's house. They were the only relatives we had in America. We ate boiled codfish and potatoes, the standard Norwegian Christmas dinner, and then Tante

Anna hid a nut in one of the bowls of rice pudding. Roy got the nut (I think she put it there on purpose) and so he received the prize of the marzipan pig. Then Pa dressed up like Santa, but the pillow kept falling out of his shirt and his beard kept winding up on his ear. There weren't many presents because we never had much money, but we had fun, and there was a warm, safe feeling.

But then I thought of what Christmas must have been like for Ma when she first came to America. She had me, but no husband, and her baby had died on the boat. I didn't understand how my real father could have left Ma—left us—like that.

I looked at Jacob, and I wondered if I could ever tell him these things. Could I trust him enough to hold my secrets?

At the lake that day, one of the lifeguards caught Audrey's fancy, and she spent the afternoon making eyes at him. Boots had it all figured out. As the two of them goggled at each other, Boots cleared her throat and called out to the lifeguard, "Shouldn't you be watching the lake?"

After our picnic lunch, Jacob took me to a private part of the lake. He helped me put my face in the water and blow bubbles out my nose. He said I had to stop being such a chicken when I swam. Soon I was able to go completely under, and by the end of the day I was diving.

When Pa saw me dive off the board, he ran to the shore, picked me up, and twirled me around. We laughed and laughed till our sides hurt. Roy trotted down with his bucket and dumped water on my head. After Pa tossed Roy into the lake, he hoisted Jacob over his shoulder, ran to the end of the diving board, and pitched him in, too.

The lifeguard blew his whistle at Pa and yelled, "No roughhousing, sir!"

Pa shouted back so everyone could hear, "Oh, we're just having some fun. Go on back to your little honey." He raised his eyebrows at Audrey, and everyone laughed—everyone that is, except Audrey and the lifeguard. It really made Boots's day.

sixteen

the spillway

After a couple of weeks in the Catskill Mountains, Jacob said he should have been born and raised in the country. He loved the grass and the hills and the animals—even the bugs—and he didn't mind the smell of chicken coops or cow manure.

Pa was a city boy, and he said all that fresh air and quiet made him stir-crazy, so he drove us into town just about every day. The year before, he had taken me alone and let me do some driving, but this year Roy and Jacob came along. I was relieved in a way, since I was still nervous around Pa. Jacob and I took turns behind the wheel, and Roy promised he wouldn't say a word to Ma about it.

In town, Pa picked up the newspaper and a few things for Ma; then he gave us each a nickel for rock candy. We'd suck on that stuff all day long. Ma scolded him, saying it was going to rot our teeth, but he kept on buying it for us. Pa was like that: stubborn as a mule. Also, he said he'd never let a woman boss him around.

At the house, when Jacob wasn't helping with chores or horsing around with me and Roy, he was spending time with Mrs. Breuger. He visited her every night and played with the black-nosed kitten. One night she told him to name the cat because it now belonged to him. He named it Bingo.

After two weeks, Pa had to go back to his tugboat because he couldn't afford any more time off. He hugged us good-bye and, at the same time, slipped us some money for rock candy; then Ma drove him to the boatyard. She was going to be gone the whole morning, so Roy, Jacob, and I made a plan to visit the spillway. Ma thought it was a dangerous place, so we conveniently forgot to mention it to her.

The spillway was more than a swimming hole; it was a secret lagoon, surrounded by rocky cliffs and waterfalls. We packed a lunch and set out on our journey. It was a five-mile walk, but the morning breeze was cool and tingly, so it didn't seem so long. When we saw the huge reservoir of water in the distance, surrounded by mountains that looked like broccoli tops sitting in the sky, we knew we were almost there.

We climbed through the woods until we reached the warm, smooth bedrock. The water that ran into the spillway was an overflow from the reservoir. Icy streams raced through channels and disappeared over the edge of the cliff. I dipped my toes into a slower, gurgling stream, and it sent shivers up my spine.

Jacob and Roy went to investigate the place, while I lay, belly down, on a flat rock. The sun felt good on my back. After a while I looked up and saw the two of them standing at the edge of the cliff, water crashing all around them. They were glancing my way and grinning.

I scrambled to my feet and ran to them. "No way! Are you guys out of your minds, or what? You're gonna get yourselves killed!"

"Oh, come on, Judy," Roy said. "We just wanna have some fun."

I was petrified of that cliff. It was steep, and the water crashed along its sides and made my head spin. As Roy and Jacob began to climb down, I ran to the side and hollered at them. "You just wait till Ma finds out!" They laughed, knowing I'd never tell Ma.

The cliff had various ledges, and I watched Jacob lead Roy to each one, carefully guiding his footsteps. I closed my eyes and prayed harder than I ever had before. When they reached the bottom and began to swim, they hooted and hollered like two hillbillies. I took a deep breath and went back to my place on the rock. I was exhausted.

About ten minutes later, Jacob came up behind me. I turned and saw that he was alone. "Where's Roy?" I asked.

"Judy, calm down. He's waiting for you at the bottom."

"You left him there?"

"Roy's fine." Jacob held out his hand. "Come on."

"Oh, no. You're not taking me down there." My heart started thumping wildly.

"Judy, it's easy. It looks a lot scarier than it is, trust me."

I glanced toward the cliff and swallowed hard.

"It's incredible," Jacob said. "I really want you to see it. I promise, I'll stay with you the whole time." He took my hand. "You know I'd never let anything happen to you."

I don't know what came over me that day, but I let Jacob take me down the cliff. When I reached the bottom and lowered myself into the pool of water, I looked at his face smiling down at me. Something passed between us—something I couldn't put into words.

I swam to a smooth, round rock and hoisted myself onto it. I pulled my knees to my chest and watched Jacob and Roy cannonball into the water. I looked around at the mountains and the great big sky and the rushing water. The beauty of it all wrapped itself around me like a warm blanket.

A waterfall near the top of the cliff caught my eye. The sun was shining through it, making a rainbow. For a split second, I thought that waterfall was telling me something. Then I heard Jacob's voice. He was calling from the other side of the lagoon. His arms were spread out to the sky. "Judy! Isn't this great?"

I stood up on the rock beneath me, reached out my arms, and closed my eyes. The sun beat down on my face and I wasn't sure how long I stood there. When I opened my eyes, Jacob was spinning around, laughing. I started to laugh, too, and in that moment I felt so light; I think I understood what the waterfall was telling me.

"What the heck are you guys doing?" Roy called out from the side of the cliff. He shook his head and cannon-balled in.

Jacob swam over to me and hopped onto the rock. We sat down together. He was breathing hard and shivering. I showed him the waterfall. He said, "That's our waterfall," and then leaned over and kissed me. I wasn't expecting it, so my lips didn't have a chance to kiss him back. I looked at him, startled. My cheeks burned, and my insides trembled. I turned to see if Roy was watching, but he was chasing pollywogs.

"I was waiting to kiss you after your pa left," Jacob said. "I wouldn't have been able to look him in the face." I laughed, and the next time Roy jumped into the water, I kissed Jacob back.

seventeen

mrs. breuger

The next day, Jacob convinced me and Roy to pay Mrs. Breuger a visit. I made sure I wore my Keds. I didn't want her examining my toenails.

"Come in, Jacob," Mrs. Breuger called with her rattly voice. She hobbled to the door, and when she saw the three of us, not only her head, but her whole body shook. "Oh, what a surprise! Judy and Roy, I'm so glad you came." A huge smile crinkled her face, and she used her leathery hands to pull us into the kitchen. The smell of mothballs wafted through the air.

"What's that smell?" Roy asked, wrinkling up his nose. I elbowed him in the ribs.

"Oh," Mrs. Breuger said, "it's my cookies. You came just in time; they're still warm."

"That's not what I'm—" Roy began, but I elbowed him again, harder.

We sat down at the table, and as Roy chewed his cookie, he gazed intently at Mrs. Breuger. "How old are you?" he asked.

I glared at him. "Roy, that's not polite."

"Oh, I don't mind," Mrs. Breuger said. "How old do you think I am?"

Roy stopped chewing, knitted his brows together, and said, "One hundred and fifteen." I choked on my cookie and Jacob laughed.

Mrs. Breuger pounded her fist on the table and shook with laughter. "How did you know?" she said.

"You mean I guessed right?" Roy asked.

"Right on the nose," she said, placing one of her bony fingers on the tip of Roy's nose. She looked over at me and Jacob and winked. I supposed she was kidding, but I wasn't quite sure.

Mrs. Breuger's kitchen was cluttered with all kinds of stuff. It made me think of the junk man in the city, pushing his cart up and down the streets, collecting everyone's junk to sell at the junkyard. He'd have a heyday at Mrs. Breuger's.

Plastered all over her kitchen walls were photographs, most of them tinged yellow with their edges peeling down. As we ate our cookies, I studied the photos. "Oh, you like my pictures!" Mrs. Breuger screeched.

I nearly jumped out of my skin. "Yes, I do. Who are the people in them?"

"Why, my family, of course," she said. "Here, let me show you."

"You have *kids*?" Roy asked with his mouth full of mashed cookies.

She smiled at Roy. "Yes, but none as ornery as you." Mrs. Breuger yanked me out of my seat and showed me photos of her seven children, eighteen grandchildren, and four great-grandchildren. Her eyes filled with tears when we came to a picture of Mr. Breuger. "That's my Walter," she said. "The good Lord saw fit to take him ten years ago, but he's right here—in my heart—as close as ever." She pressed her hand to her chest.

We stayed with Mrs. Breuger for a good part of the day, and our visit made her rattle and shake with happiness. I felt bad about the way I'd shunned her in the past. I realized she was just a sweet old lady who needed some company. It took Jacob to show me how wrong I'd been. Mrs. Breuger wound up giving Roy a cat, too. It had orange and black stripes, so Roy named it Tiger.

That evening, after supper, Jacob and I took a walk along the road and he asked me if I would be his girlfriend. My stomach started flopping around. I liked the idea, but I was nervous about it. I'd never been anyone's girlfriend, and I wasn't quite sure what to do.

"Okay," I said. "But I don't think I want Ma or Roy to know. Can we keep it a secret, at least for a while?"

Jacob smiled and reached for my hand. He held it in a special way, with his fingers laced into mine. It felt really good. Our arms swung gently back and forth. "Sure," he said. "I won't say anything. It can be *our* secret."

When Jacob said that, I started to wonder if I should open up to him—tell him what I'd been hiding about me and my family. Maybe sharing it with someone would be good, I thought. But if I brought it up, things might be spoiled, and right then everything seemed so perfect. Maybe I'd just ask a question and see what happened. "Hey, Jacob," I said. "Have your parents ever kept a secret from you? I mean something really big?"

He looked at me in a strange way.

I shrugged and looked down. "I was just wondering."

He thought for a while. "Well, I don't know, but I do remember when my sister Ingrid was dating a Catholic guy. She kept that a secret for a while."

"Really? What happened?"

"Some nosy lady at church called my mother. She said she saw Ingrid with Bobby Finnegan, who went to St. Joseph's Catholic Church, and they were holding hands. So when my mother asked Ingrid about it, Ingrid said they already broke up."

I smiled. "Was it true?"

"I don't know."

We both laughed, and then Jacob said, "But why are you asking me about parents and secrets?"

"No reason," I said. But I didn't sound too convincing.

"You know, you act kind of strange around your parents sometimes."

I looked at him. "What do you mean?"

"Well, like that time when your mother said you could take art lessons, and you just walked away. And sometimes you get all stiff when your father gives you a hug."

"No I don't."

"Yeah, you do."

We walked a bit farther. I didn't want to talk about this anymore, so I was quiet and focused on how Jacob's hand felt in mine. I thought it was funny, being his girlfriend now—just the day before, we were friends. Then I thought of something. "Jacob? Have you ever had a girlfriend?"

He didn't say anything for a minute. "Well, sort of. Jenny Olsen. But that was about a year ago."

"Jenny Olsen?" I said. "I didn't know that."

"Well, it only lasted three weeks."

Jenny was in my math class in seventh grade. All the boys thought she was cute, but if you asked me, she was a little short on brains. Also, she'd been having boyfriends since fifth grade, and I figured she was pretty experienced. "Did you ever kiss her?"

"Um . . . sort of."

"How can you *sort of* kiss someone?"

"I don't know," he said. "Forget about it. I don't like her anymore. I like you." He looked me in the eye and gave my hand a squeeze.

That made me feel a little better. We walked some

more, but I kept thinking about Jenny. "Jenny Olsen's kind of fat," I said.

Jacob laughed and pulled me toward him. "Will you forget about Jenny Olsen!"

We still had an hour of daylight, so we hopped the fence and headed to the clearing in the woods. Before we reached the tire swing and the bathtub, Jacob stopped.

"What is it?" I said.

He touched the side of my face and brushed back my hair. My heart started pounding; it was so loud I was sure Jacob could hear it. My legs felt all wobbly. He leaned forward and pressed his lips gently to mine. My eyes closed. I couldn't believe how soft his mouth was. It felt even better than the kiss at the spillway.

Jacob let go and whispered in my ear. "What's today?"

"August fifteenth. Why?"

He stepped back and smiled. "Watch this." He led me to the big oak tree in the middle of the clearing. He pulled out his pocketknife and carved into the tree:

JACOB & JUDY
8-15-44

When he was done, I ran my fingers over it. I liked the way it looked. Then I thought about the date. "We've only got two more weeks in the Catskills," I said.

Jacob sighed and took my hand. "I don't want to go back. I wish we could stay here forever."

We headed to the tire swing; I hopped on and Jacob spun me in circles. I laughed really hard, and when I couldn't stand it anymore, he stopped the swing and climbed on with me. We swung gently, side to side, holding hands and listening to the crickets. We got home right at dark, and Ma had dessert for us. While we sat in the kitchen eating ice cream with Roy, Jacob kept brushing his bare feet against mine under the table.

"Stop it," I whispered. I pushed his foot away and we both started to giggle.

"What the heck's the matter with you guys?" Roy said. "What's so funny?"

"Nothing," I said, waving my spoon at him. "Just eat."

Roy screwed up his face. "If nothing's funny, then what are you two laughing about?"

Ma had been washing dishes at the sink. She turned around and looked back and forth between Jacob and me. A big smile spread across her face. "Oh, Roy," she said, "can't you see?"

So much for keeping *that* a secret.

That night, I wrote Annette a letter and told her about Jacob and me. A week later, she wrote back and said the same thing had happened with her and Andy. They'd kissed and everything. Olaf didn't speak to her for a few days, but after a while he got over it. She had told Harold about me and Jacob, and he had just said, "That figures."

In the letter Annette mentioned double-dating when

we got back, and all of a sudden I felt so grown up. I could hardly fall asleep that night, thinking about all the things we'd do together when we got back to Brooklyn.

At the lake the next day, while Roy was busy building a dam, Jacob and I slipped away together. We passed the diving board, waded through swampy water, and came to a deserted part of the lake. We walked along the sandy edge, hand in hand. I was hoping for a kiss before we had to go back.

Then we heard footsteps behind us. We dropped hands and turned around. It was Roy. He was out of breath, and he had an angry look on his face. He stopped and put his hands on his hips. "So that's what Ma was talking about!"

"What are you doing?" I said. "Why are you following us?"

"You can't fool me! I saw you holding hands!" Roy looked at Jacob and pointed his finger at me. "You like her better than me, don't you?"

"Oh, Roy," Jacob said. He walked over, knelt down, and put his arm around Roy's shoulder. "We're still pals, you know that. But I really like your sister, too."

"Yeah, and now you're gonna spend all your time with Judy, holding hands and smooching and all that stuff." Roy looked like he was about to cry.

"It won't be so bad," Jacob said. "I'll make sure I spend plenty of time with you, too."

Roy pouted and blinked a few times. "Then will you come back with me now and help me build my dam?"

Jacob turned to me. From the look on his face I could tell Roy had suckered him in.

I glared at the two of them. "Fine," I said.

"Yay!" Roy jumped up and down, and I gave his rear end a swat.

The three of us headed back to the lake. While we were walking, I leaned into Jacob and whispered in his ear, "You owe me a kiss."

I actually made him blush.

The rest of our vacation flew by. Jacob and I slipped away to be alone as often as we could—taking walks, holding hands, stealing kisses—but a few days before our departure, he seemed to clam up. He got real quiet and went off on his own sometimes without telling me. I didn't say anything; I knew he was worried about going home, but I felt shut out. During these times, I visited my favorite spots with my sketchbook, pencils, and paints. My artwork had improved a lot over the summer, and I was pleased with my progress. Ma hadn't mentioned anything else about the art lessons, so I thought I might bring them up sometime before school started.

On the evening before our drive back to Brooklyn, Jacob sat on the front porch, stroking his cat, Bingo, and staring into space. I came and sat beside him. "Bet you can't wait to see Andy," I said.

"Yeah, I miss Andy."

"School starts in a couple of weeks. Are you excited?" I asked. He shrugged and grunted. "Listen, Jacob. I'm sure Douglas has found someone else to pick on by now."

"I'm not worried about him. It's my father. I just wish things could be different."

"Yeah," I said, "I know." Right then, I realized that my own heart hadn't been aching as much as usual. Maybe it was the magic of the country, or maybe it was Jacob who had filled the spaces inside me, but I knew it had something to do with giving. The more I gave, the more whole I felt.

The next morning, Ma shooed us out of the house and repeated her cleaning frenzy. After we loaded up the car, we said good-bye to Mrs. Breuger. I gave her a photograph of our family to add to her collection, and she gave me a hug so tight I thought I'd pop like a grape. We were a little low on gas, so Mrs. Breuger helped us out. She barely drove, and she didn't even need her three-gallon ration. On the ride home, Bingo and Tiger screeched and howled and scooted under the gas pedal. They'd never been in a car before.

"Judy!" Ma cried. "Do something about these cats!" She was a nervous wreck.

"It's okay, Ma, we'll be home soon." I placed my hands on her shoulders and rubbed out the tension. "Stop being such a worrywart, will you?" Jacob scooped up the cats and held them tightly to his chest. I looked at him and smiled, but he seemed far away. We were almost home.

eighteen
crumbled

I breathed in the city air billowing through the car window. Brooklyn air. Closing my eyes, I pictured Annette racing out her front door to greet me. I pictured Harold and Olaf playing stickball in the street, stopping their game to welcome us home. I thought about school; the first day of ninth grade was right around the corner.

Jacob's mother met him at the front door and she gave him an enormous hug. Ma and I got out of the car to say hello. Roy was asleep with Tiger in the backseat. Jacob had Bingo cupped in his hands, and he held him up for his mother to see. "Ma," he said, "let me run over to Andy's house and show him the cat."

Mrs. Jacobsen's face dropped. "Jacob," she said, "Andy's not home." She was pale and looked much thinner than I had remembered.

Ma noticed, too, because she said, "Clara, are you feeling okay?"

"Oh, I'm fine, now that my Jacob is back," she said, hugging him again, but her face was strained, and her smile was like a tight rubber band.

"Is Andy coming home soon?" Jacob asked. "I really want to see him."

"Yes, soon," she said. "Now come in and spend some time with me. We have a lot to talk about."

"Okay, Ma," he said. Mrs. Jacobsen said *tusen takk* to Ma about a hundred times for letting Jacob stay with us, and then Jacob gave Ma a big hug and headed inside. "See you tomorrow, Judy."

As I had expected, the kids on Fifty-sixth Street were out playing ball, and as we drove up the block they greeted us with cheers and whistles, waking Roy from his deep sleep. It felt good to have been missed. Harold helped us unload the car. I felt kind of funny that he knew about me and Jacob, and he kept staring at me like I'd grown two heads. When he tripped down the steps and landed on his rear, I burst out laughing.

"What's your problem?" I said. "Did you forget what I looked like or something?"

"No," he said, brushing off the seat of his pants.

"So anyway, where's Annette?" I asked, looking up and down the street.

"I think she's still at church with Andy."

"What do you mean? Today's not Sunday."

Harold looked at me in a peculiar way. "Don't you know about Andy's father? I thought that's why you came home today."

"What about Andy's father?" I asked.

"He was killed in battle." The words were like a boulder landing on my chest. "They got the letter a few days ago," Harold said. "There's a memorial service for him at church today. Me and Olaf just got back, but Annette's still there. I'm sorry, Judy, I thought you knew."

"No. I don't believe it." I ran into the house. Stupid war. Stupid, stupid war, I screamed inside my head. I ran to Ma and told her the news. She told Roy and me to change our clothes and we'd head over to the service.

"Why didn't Mrs. Jacobsen tell us about Andy's father?" I asked as we walked to church.

Ma said, "She knew Jacob would be upset. I'm sure she didn't want to tell him in front of us."

Inside the church, Jacob was sitting next to Andy in one of the pews. My eyes searched for Annette, but I couldn't find her. I had a sinking feeling. Flowers covered the platform and altar; the church organ was moaning. I looked for a casket, but then I realized there was none; Andy's father would be buried overseas.

We sat down, and I wasn't sure what to do. I looked at Ma. She had her head down and eyes closed. I looked at Roy. He was fidgeting and pulling on his shirt collar. I concentrated, trying to think about Andy's father. The problem was that I didn't remember what he looked like, and all I saw was my little sister's face. Then I said a prayer.

Andy's mother was sitting in the front pew. I saw only her back and glimpses of her profile when people came and paid their respects. She was sitting straight and erect, and she was not crying. When people greeted her, she moved rigidly and gave blank stares in their direction. She didn't seem to recognize anyone.

I began to feel queasy, so I left for the bathroom. I hung my head over the toilet and threw up until my stomach felt like it had turned inside out. I rinsed out my mouth. Then I walked out and headed to the pew where Andy and Jacob were sitting.

"Judy," Andy said as I sat down next to him. His eyes were red and swollen. I took his hand and opened my mouth, but nothing came out. I looked at Jacob; his face was pale. "Annette's at my house," Andy said. "She's taking care of my brothers. My mother . . ." He glanced in her direction. "She isn't doing well."

"I'm so sorry, Andy" was all I could say. My throat felt like it was on fire, and I wanted desperately to leave that place. "Should I go and help Annette?"

Andy nodded; I was relieved I had a place to go. I whispered good-bye to Jacob, squeezed Andy's hand, and slipped away.

When I arrived at Andy's house, Annette was sitting on the sofa, cradling Andy's brothers, rocking them and stroking their heads. I sat in the chair next to Annette and I thought back to the last time I had seen these boys—

running, laughing, throwing dirt-ball hand grenades at us. I looked at them now, all quiet. I wondered how they would make it through.

We sat in stillness for what seemed like an eternity. The youngest boy whimpered for his mother, and from time to time I could hear the middle one sucking hard on his thumb. The oldest sat very still, staring into space.

Then we heard the front door open. Andy and his mother came in; Jacob and another lady were with them. The boys jumped out of Annette's lap. "Maaa," they cried, running to her with their arms outstretched.

She marched past them; her face looked like a mask. She didn't seem to hear or even recognize them. She went to her room and closed the door. It made me think about when Ma held her arms out to me after I'd found my adoption papers. I'd shut the door on her and let her cry alone.

The youngest boy followed his mother, and when he found her door locked, he screamed and banged his head against it. Andy scooped him up in his arms, but the little boy kicked him and elbowed him in the face. Jacob grabbed the boy from Andy and held him tight. The whole thing scared me half to death.

The lady who had come in with them walked over to Jacob. She looked like Andy's mother, but older, and I figured she was Andy's aunt. She held out her hands to the little boy. He immediately flung his arms and legs around her and cried into her neck. Andy hung his head and trudged into his room; Jacob followed. The two other boys ran to their aunt and clung to her skirt. "Tante Helen," cried the oldest. "Why's Ma being so mean to us?"

"Sweetheart," she said, "Ma is very upset now. She misses your father, just like you do. Sometimes when people are sad, they don't act like themselves. But she loves you very much, and we have to give her some time. I'll be here with you till she's feeling better."

"Tante Helen," the youngest said, "is Ma gonna die, too?"

"No, no." She soothed him and kissed his forehead. "Your ma will always be here. I promise."

As I watched this happen, I thought again of my own mother and how her whole world must have crumbled, just like Andy's mother's had, when she came to America with no husband, an empty cradle, and me. I wondered who was there to pick me up and tell me everything would be okay. Was it Pa who did that? Maybe. I wished I could remember.

Annette and I tiptoed toward Andy's room. "Girls," Tante Helen said, "thank you so much for taking care of the boys. You've been very kind."

I wanted to run away and never set foot in that house again. There was too much sadness. I could hardly stand it. But Annette said, "We'll be back tomorrow." At that moment I realized something about Annette. She was strong, and brave—much braver than me.

Tante Helen smiled at us. "I think I may need your help. Thank you."

We went into Andy's room. He and Jacob were sitting

on the bed, talking quietly. Andy stood up and hugged Annette; he whispered something in her ear and she nodded. Then he walked the three of us to the door and said good-bye; we said we'd see him in the morning.

We stepped outside, and the cool air reminded me that autumn was coming. Autumn, I thought. It was the time when everything started to die. Goose bumps prickled up my arms and legs. "I'm cold," I said to Jacob. He put his arm around me, and then he walked me and Annette home. None of us said much. I glanced at Annette and felt bad that she was alone.

Ma made me a grilled cheese sandwich when I got back, and Roy snuggled up next to me on the sofa while I ate. Tiger hopped onto Roy's lap, purring and sniffing at my food. Roy felt warm and good, and I didn't push him away like I normally did. He looked up at me with eyes that seemed to ask a million questions. I didn't have the answer to any of them.

nineteen
charlie

Andy's mother got worse. When the three of us went to baby-sit and help out the next day, she was half-dressed and her hair was tangled and greasy. When I walked past the bathroom, I saw her by the mirror, smearing on lipstick with a shaky hand. When she was finished, it looked like she had colored outside the lines with a red crayon. Then she sat on the sofa and pushed her lips together for about ten minutes. She didn't talk to anyone, and she just picked at the food Tante Helen put in front of her. I heard Tante Helen use the term "nervous breakdown" a few times when she spoke to someone on the phone.

Andy's mother did another strange thing, and it scared

me clear out of my mind. She took out an ice pick and sat down with it at the kitchen table. She just sat there, rolling it around in her hands. I almost stopped breathing, because I thought she was going to stab herself with it. Tante Helen and Andy both tried to take it from her, but she wouldn't let it go. She mumbled as she twirled it around, and I listened real close. I knew eavesdropping wasn't exactly polite, but she was talking to an ice pick, and I needed to be prepared for anything.

"I didn't know it was out on the table," she said. "Can you fix his eye? Oh, God, it's bleeding so much. I'm so sorry, my baby, my little Andy. I'm so sorry."

Andy wrapped his arms around his mother and said, "It's okay, Ma; it wasn't your fault. It was an accident. It happened a long time ago, and I'm fine now. Please let me have that." She finally released the ice pick, and Andy took it out of the room. Now I knew why Andy had a glass eye. And his poor mother obviously blamed herself.

Things continued the same way for about a week. Jacob, Annette, and I went over every day to baby-sit. We helped Andy with some chores around the house, too, but mostly we were there to support him and keep him company. Andy's mother lay in bed most of the time, and she refused to shower. She started to smell bad. Tante Helen kept offering her food, but she barely ate. Then she stopped speaking.

By the end of the week, Andy's brothers were getting hard to control. They ran around the house, screaming, fighting, and throwing things. One day Andy spanked all three of them with a wooden paddle and sent them to their rooms. Tante Helen looked worried. She told the four of us to go out and get some fresh air; we needed a break.

We walked along the street, hand in hand, Annette and Andy in front, Jacob and me behind. We decided to go to the ice cream parlor. I was glad to get out, but it wasn't the way I had pictured our first double date. We sat down in a booth and ordered sodas. None of us were smiling. Then Andy told us the news.

"There's something I have to tell you guys," he said. He stared down at the table. "Tante Helen says we have to move in with her for a while. She has a big house out on Long Island, and she thinks my mother can get better there."

Annette gasped. "Oh, no, Andy. Don't say that. You can't go." She turned to us. "We'll help—you'll see, she'll be all right." She reached for his hand and started to breathe real fast.

Andy took her hand and looked at her sadly. "Tante Helen's already decided. She's going to rent out our house for a while; she even knows a family who wants it. We're leaving in a few days."

"Hey, you can stay with me, Andy," Jacob said. "At my house. We have room. My mother will say it's okay, I know she will."

Andy looked up at the three of us. He pulled Annette close to him. "I can't leave my mother. I have to go with them and help out. But she'll get better, and we'll come back real soon."

Annette's eyes started to well up. She put her head on Andy's shoulder.

117

"I'll write you all the time," Andy said to her.

The four of us were inseparable those last few days until it was time to say good-bye. Then Tante Helen gathered Andy's family up under her wings and carted them off to Long Island. She said her house had plenty of room, the schools were good, and she'd see to it that her sister got better. Andy told us again that he'd be back soon, and not to worry.

Two days later, the Gundersens moved into Andy's house. They had a whole slew of kids, and the oldest was Charlie. We knew him because he had gone to Pershing Junior High, like us. The girls at school thought he was handsome. I thought he was full of himself, always shooting off his mouth and acting tough. But for some reason, Jacob seemed to think he was okay.

It was hard after Andy left. Jacob and Annette moped around a lot. I looked for ways to cheer them up, but nothing seemed to help.

"How about a game of stickball?" I said one afternoon. We were sitting on Jacob's stoop. It was the last Saturday before school started. "We can call for Harold and Olaf and see if they want to play."

Jacob shrugged. "Okay. I haven't seen those guys in a while."

Annette agreed. "Yeah, maybe it'll take my mind off of Andy."

Just then Jacob's mother poked her head out the window. "Jacob," she called. "Would you please run to the store for me? I need a loaf of rye and some *bolle* from Olsen's."

"Okay, Ma, I'll be right there." He stood up and said to us, "I'll meet you on your block in just a little while."

Annette and I went home and called for Harold and Olaf; then Roy and Pauley came out and asked if they could play. "You can be the ball boys," I said. That was the job we always gave Roy and Pauley. They would stand at the bottom of the street and catch the balls that got past us. If the balls went down the sewers, it was their job to fish them out.

"Oh, come on, Judy," Roy said. "Let us play a real game for once." He whined and carried on.

"Yeah, give 'em a chance, Judy," Olaf said.

"Oh, all right."

We played a game of stoopball and waited for Jacob. Then Annette pointed down the street. "Who's that with Jacob?" she said.

There were three kids walking toward us. Harold squinted and said, "It's that bigmouthed kid, Charlie Gundersen, the one who moved into Andy's house. The other one is his friend Bobby Parker."

"Why is Jacob bringing them around?" Olaf said.

Then Charlie called out to us, "Hey! Are you ready to get your rear ends whipped?"

"Who does he think he is?" Roy said.

When they reached us, Jacob said, "Hey, guys, Charlie and Bobby are gonna play a game with us."

"Yeah," Charlie said. "The three of us against all of you. That'd be about even." He elbowed Bobby and they started to laugh.

Roy piped up. "That's not fair. I want to be on Jacob's team."

"Who's the twerp?" Charlie said.

I stepped right up to him. "That's my brother, Charlie, so watch your mouth!"

"Whoa!" Charlie said, holding up both hands. "Take it easy; I was just kidding around."

Jacob looked embarrassed. He patted Roy's head. "You can be on my team, Roy."

Roy crossed his arms over his chest and glared at Charlie.

"How 'bout we choose up sides?" Annette said.

And that's what we did. It was Charlie, Bobby, Olaf, and Pauley against Jacob, Harold, Annette, Roy, and me. The first time Charlie got up to bat, he held his chin in the air and said, "I'll show you how it's done." The next time, he stepped to the plate and said, "Just watch me; you'll catch on." I thought Harold was going to pop him before the end of that stickball game.

When we finished playing, Charlie said, "Hey, whadaya say we go to the movies?"

All of us got quiet. Besides the no-dancing and no-cursing rules, Norwegian Lutherans were generally not allowed to go to the movies. Sometimes Pa would sneak me into an old Charlie Chaplin film, but he always said not to tell Ma. She was pretty strict about those things.

"I don't know," Harold said. "I don't have any money."

Olaf pulled out his pockets. "Yeah, me neither."

"You don't need money," Charlie said. "Me and Bobby sneak in all the time. We never get caught. How 'bout you, Jacob? You wanna go?"

Jacob looked at me. "Do you want to go, Judy?" He seemed very uncomfortable.

Before I could say anything, Roy blurted out, "Judy's not allowed to go to the movies."

Charlie and Bobby looked at each other and burst out laughing.

My face started to burn. "Get in the house, Roy!" I yelled. "I've had enough of you!"

Roy's face crumpled. "I'm tellin' Ma!" He ran into the house. By this time Charlie and Bobby were practically on the floor.

"Hey," Bobby said to Charlie and Jacob, "*Pin Up Girl* with Betty Grable is playing at the Center Theatre." He lifted his eyebrows a few times. "I'd like to see that one."

"I don't know," Jacob said. "How about *Lifeboat*? That's the new Alfred Hitchcock movie."

My throat swelled up and my eyes started to sting. I'd never be able to see either of those movies, and it looked like Jacob was going to choose Charlie and Bobby over me.

I looked at Harold and Olaf. They had inched away from the rest of us. I guess they weren't about to go sneaking into the movies. If their parents found out, they'd be in big trouble.

A few minutes later, Roy came barreling out the door,

grinning from ear to ear. "Judy, guess what! Ma said we can see *Snow White and the Seven Dwarfs*! She gave us money and everything!"

That really set Charlie and Bobby off. By this time Jacob was laughing with them. Annette took my arm and pulled me aside. "Just ignore them," she said. She glanced at the three of them. "What's gotten into Jacob?"

So, that afternoon, Jacob went with Charlie and Bobby to see *Pin Up Girl* at the Center Theatre, and I took Roy to see *Snow White* at the Berkshire. Pauley came with us. Being Irish Catholic, his mother didn't care one way or the other about movies. The only thing the Catholics seemed to care about was the no-meat-on-Friday rule. I thought the Norwegians would be better off with that one, since we were always eating fish anyway.

While Roy, Pauley, and I walked to the theater, Roy kept saying, "I can't believe Ma is letting us see a movie!" Actually, I was surprised myself. That was a big step for Ma. *Snow White* turned out to be pretty good—it was a lot better than Charlie Chaplin—but I couldn't stop thinking about the way Jacob had treated me. He'd never acted that way before.

twenty
sunday dress

The next day was Sunday. I slipped into my one and only Sunday dress, the one Ma had made for me a year ago. Since the war, there had been a shortage of dresses, and the few you could buy were very expensive. No one had nylon stockings, either, because the army needed nylon for parachutes and gunpowder bags. Ma had to wear makeup on her legs to cover her spider veins.

I looked at myself in the mirror. I'd never thought much about my dress, but now the sleeves looked too puffy, and the top made my chest seem even flatter than it was. I looked, well, babyish. I sighed and turned away. There was nothing I could do now. I tied my saddle shoes and headed out the door.

"Bye, Ma, I'm leaving," I called.

"Okay, Judy. We'll see you after church." Ma was getting Roy ready for Sunday school, and then she and Pa would go to the Norwegian service. I went with my friends to the English service in the building next door. I purposely left a little early so I could wait for Jacob in front of the church. I called for Annette, but she wasn't ready, so I said I'd meet her there.

When Jacob arrived, I waved to him. He gave me a tense smile and touched my elbow, and we walked in. We sat close together in the pew, and while the pastor talked I slid my hand into Jacob's. Maybe I had overreacted. Maybe things would go back to normal.

After the service everyone was milling around outside, saying hello to friends and family. I saw Jacob's parents coming out of the Norwegian service. I was surprised, because I'd never seen his father in church before.

"Your father's here," I said.

Jacob looked into the crowd, and when he saw his parents, he frowned. Then I noticed that Mrs. Jacobsen didn't look right. Her face was pale and strained, and she was a little stooped over. Jacob took my hand and led me away. He was quiet as we walked down the street.

"What's the matter?" I said.

He sighed. "It's my mother. She's been sick and they won't tell me what's wrong. My father took her to the hospital last week. He said the doctors ran some tests."

"Oh." I squeezed his hand. I felt bad and I didn't know what to say. "Well, I'm sure she'll be okay. They'll give her some medicine or something."

Jacob looked worried. "I hope so, but I don't know. There's a lot of strange things going on at home. My sisters are moving back in with us. They quit their jobs at the factory and they've been doing stuff around the house. And they said my father stopped drinking. I didn't believe them at first, but then I saw it for myself. He came straight home from his fishing trip and didn't go to the bars."

"Well, that's really good about your father."

Jacob shrugged. "I guess he's doing it for my mother. I guess that's why he's in church, too."

"You should be glad, Jacob," I said. "Maybe things will change now."

"We'll see. I'm just worried about my mother."

We walked along Eighth Avenue, and when we got to Jacob's corner, we saw his cat, Bingo, darting under a parked car. "He's not supposed to be out," Jacob said.

We ran down the street to catch him. While we poked our heads under the car, Charlie came out of his house with a football under his arm.

"Hey, Jacob," he called. "Whatcha doin'?"

Jacob looked up. "Hey, Charlie. Just trying to get my cat."

I grabbed Bingo by the back of his neck and pulled him out. He started yowling. I stood up and Charlie sneered at me.

"You tryin' to kill that cat, Judy?" Charlie said. He laughed and scoped me up and down. I thought about my dress and how ridiculous I looked. I handed the cat to Jacob. Charlie tossed the football in the air and caught it. "Hey, you wanna play some football, buddy?"

Jacob stroked Bingo and calmed him down. "Sure, Charlie. I just got to put the cat inside and change my clothes." Then Jacob turned to me. "Um, maybe I'll see you later, Judy, okay?"

My throat tightened. Jacob looked down and kicked a rock. I could barely speak. "Sure," I said. "I'll see you later." I turned and walked up the street. A huge pain spread from my throat to my chest. When I rounded the corner, I saw Harold, Olaf, and Annette walking on the avenue. I slowed down. I didn't want to talk to anyone. I just wanted to be alone.

I waited for Jacob that afternoon, but he never came to see me. After a while, I got tired of staring at the walls, so I went over to Annette's house and told her what had happened. Then the two of us moped around because she was missing Andy, too.

"It was gonna be so fun," she said. "Me and Andy, you and Jacob; and now look. I wish Andy didn't have to move away."

"And I wish Charlie never moved in," I said. "He's ruined everything."

Annette stared into space for a while and rubbed her

chin. "You know, Judy, maybe you need to try something a little different."

"What do you mean?" I said.

"You know, to get Jacob to pay attention to you. I have an idea."

"What kind of idea?" I wasn't sure I liked the sound of this.

"You'll see, I'm gonna help you out. I got a plan."

twenty-one

handball

The next day we started school. Phase one of Annette's plan was for me to act cool around Jacob and play hard to get. This was easy, since he pretty much ignored me the entire day.

Jacob was in two of my classes—history and English—and I was happy to see we had lunch together. But then Charlie walked into the lunchroom, and that spoiled everything. Charlie strutted around with a bunch of his friends, then plopped himself next to Jacob. I noticed a group of popular girls turning their heads and staring at the two of them. I heard whispers like "What did Charlie say?" and "What did Jacob do?" It was all pretty nauseating. I parked myself next to Annette and pretended not to notice.

Later that afternoon, we heard rumors that Douglas O'Reilly was after Jacob again. That's when Charlie stepped in as Jacob's personal bodyguard. I overheard Charlie in the hallway. "I ain't gonna let that creep O'Reilly push my buddy around." After school, Charlie got a bunch of his friends together and took care of Douglas. I wasn't around to see it, but I heard about it the next day. The news was flying all over school.

I continued to act cool toward Jacob for the next few days, but Annette's plan wasn't working. He barely spoke to me at all. Then Annette said we needed to put phase two into action. She called it "Fight for Your Man."

While we were walking home from school the following day, Annette spotted Jacob and Charlie a block ahead of us. "Judy, look, there they are. Now's your chance."

"Annette, I don't think this is a good idea." But before I knew it, she was calling to them. She grabbed my arm and pulled me along.

Charlie said hi to Annette; then he sneered at me. Jacob sort of grunted at the two of us and continued walking.

"Hey, did you hear what I did to that creep Douglas O'Reilly?" Charlie said.

"We heard something about it," Annette said. "But no details."

"Well, I beat the livin' daylights out of him when I heard he was after my friend here."

"It's about time someone put that kid in his place," Annette said. "I'm glad you did it, Charlie." Jacob walked along with his head down, not saying a word.

I looked at Charlie. "I don't think that's the last you'll see of Douglas."

"Oh yeah? Well, you didn't see the damage yet. Wait till you see his face. In fact, he may not even have a face left if he tries to mess with my buddy again."

"Aren't you the tough guy?" I mumbled under my breath.

When we came to our corner, Annette said, "Hey, do you all want to meet at the schoolyard and play some handball or something?"

"All right," Charlie said, shrugging. "I'll bring some of my other friends around, too. How about four o'clock?"

"Sounds good," Annette said. "See ya later."

We walked up the street, and I was steamed. "Annette, what if I don't feel like playing handball with them? Did you ever think of that?"

"Gosh, Judy, I'm just trying to help. And you love handball. Think about it. Maybe now you'll get a chance to talk to Jacob."

"I don't know, Annette. I don't even know what to say to him anymore."

She looped her arm into mine. "Come on, Judy. It's all gonna work out."

We went home and changed; then we stopped at Harold's house and asked if he and Olaf wanted to come along.

"No way," Harold said. "I ain't gonna torture my ears listening to that windbag. Tell Jacob I said hi, and then tell him to get rid of that kid."

When Annette and I got to the handball courts, Jacob and Charlie hadn't arrived yet. The courts were full, so we had to challenge two boys for control of the court. We won easily, then hit the ball around, waiting for the others to show up. From a distance Annette spotted them. They were walking with some troublemaking kids from school. A few were smoking cigarettes. Several girls with tight clothes and bright red lipstick were tagging along, laughing and talking real loud.

"Annette, let's leave," I said. "Let's get out of here before they see us."

"We can't leave now, Judy. It'll be okay. Just relax."

"Look at the kids Charlie's bringing with him. You wanna hang around with them?" I asked.

Just then Charlie caught sight of us. "Hey! Annette's holding the court for us. Way to go, Annette!" he shouted.

Annette waved them on. I wanted to leave so badly, but it was too late. I watched Jacob as he walked toward us. A girl was giggling alongside him and tugging on his arm. The whole gang hopped onto the court, with Charlie in the lead.

"Okay," Charlie said. "Me and Jacob challenge Joe and Mike." The girls squealed and cheered them on.

Annette spoke up. "Okay, Charlie, but me and Judy get winners."

"You bet," he said, winking at her.

Charlie's friends sat down to watch the game, and I

dragged Annette to the other side of the court. The group of girls began whispering to each other and pointing in our direction. After Jacob and Charlie won the first game, Charlie held up the ball and said, "Okay, bring on the next suckers!" A couple of boys jumped up, but Jacob stopped them.

"We're playing Judy and Annette," he said, holding out his hand.

The girls started giggling, and Charlie moaned. "Jacob," he said, "let's at *least* even out the sides. How about me and Annette against you and Judy?"

I was ready to wring that kid's neck. "Sorry, Charlie," I said, "but Annette and I will *kill* the two of you." I took the ball from his hands. "Let's play."

"Fine," Charlie said. He placed his hands on his hips and batted his eyelashes to mock me. "I just thought you wanted to play on Jacob's team." At that, the girls burst out laughing. I was beyond mad—beyond furious. I got up to serve, and I slammed the ball so hard that Charlie couldn't return it. We scored the first point.

"All right," Charlie said, "so you girls are serious players, huh? Serve it again; we were just warming up."

I glanced at Jacob; his expression seemed blank. I served again, and during the next few rallies he returned every ball that came to him in a steady, rhythmic way. Charlie was the one who kept going for winners and then messing up.

Annette and I scored ten points in a row, and by that time Charlie was getting steamed. All the girls were sitting quietly, like they were waiting for an explosion.

"Maybe we should stop playing," Jacob said as he stood bouncing the ball. It was his turn to serve.

Everyone looked at him like he was crazy, but I just watched.

"Are you joking?" Annette said. "You think we're gonna quit when we're this far ahead?"

"We can do it, Jacob," Charlie said. "Come on, just serve the ball."

Jacob hesitated at first, but when he started to play, he stroked the ball harder than before and with more accuracy. He never looked at me once during that time. He and Charlie were able to score some points, but in the end Annette and I won 15 to 9.

After the game, Charlie looked at us and smirked. "You think I was playing my hardest? Come on, we gave you that game."

That was too much for Annette. "Oh yeah, Mr. Hotshot," she said. "Play us again—as hard as you can—and we'll still slaughter you." While Annette let off steam, I looked at Jacob, hoping to see something familiar in his eyes. He turned away from me, and one of the girls walked over to him and put her arm through his.

I ran out of the park as fast as I could. I heard Annette calling after me, but I didn't stop. I just kept running and running as tears poured down my face.

twenty-two
graves

That night, I sat on the sofa trying to study the war map in *The New York Times*. I traced my fingers over the dotted lines and the solid lines, the Allies versus the Axis. We had to keep track of the war for history class, and it was all becoming a blur. Then I heard a loud banging at the front door. "Judy! Mr. and Mrs. Strand!"

I ran to the door with Pa behind me. When I opened it, Jacob stood holding Bingo; the cat was limp in his arms, blood trickling down the fur on the side of his mouth. Jacob was breathing heavily. "My father ran over him with the car," he said. "Can you do anything?"

Pa told Jacob to come in. He took the cat from Jacob's arms and examined it. Ma ran and got an old blanket to keep the cat warm.

"Jacob," Pa said, "I'm sorry. It looks like your cat is dying. He's bleeding inside his belly." He took the blanket from Ma. "Let's wrap him up and you can hold him for a while. He's unconscious, so he's not in pain anymore." Pa wrapped Bingo in the blanket, and Jacob held the cat close to his body. We all sat down in the living room together. Tiger jumped up and sniffed at the bloody cat. Roy held him back and started crying.

"My father ran him over," Jacob said, staring straight ahead at the wall. "He was drunk, and he ran him over."

We buried Bingo in the little patch of our garden that night. Pa walked Jacob home and I tried to finish studying, but the words and lines got jumbled, and all I saw were graves: war graves, ocean graves, graves of broken liquor bottles, kitten graves, and mice graves scattered with flowers.

While I slept that night, the faceless man with dark hair haunted me. This time he was standing in a graveyard. I watched as he walked deeper and deeper into the ground until he disappeared. I wanted to tell him something, but the words were stuck in my throat. I woke up in a cold sweat, shivering and shaking. For the rest of the night I lay there, wondering if my real father was dead.

At school the next day, I tried to talk to Jacob. I thought

maybe he'd confide in me now after what had happened the night before. But I never got the chance; he avoided me in class, and every other minute Charlie was right by his side. I rode my bike to Jacob's street later that afternoon, but from the corner I could hear Charlie's big mouth: "Okay, guys, watch how it's done." I turned my bike around and rode home.

That night after dinner, while Roy listened to *The Lone Ranger* on the radio, I tiptoed into the kitchen to talk to Ma. I pulled out a chair and sat down.

"What's the matter with Jacob's mother?" I said. I wasn't sure how Ma would respond, because she was always telling us to mind our own business.

Ma frowned and whisked something in a bowl. "I'm not sure, Judy. She hasn't been well, but she won't tell me what it is. She says she doesn't want anyone to worry."

"Well, Jacob's real worried about her. They won't tell him what's wrong, either."

"Yes, well, that doesn't surprise me, Judy."

I sat there awhile longer. Ma poured batter into a pan. "And what about Jacob's father?" I said. "I thought he wasn't drinking anymore. What happened to that?"

Ma stopped what she was doing and sighed deeply. She turned to me. "It's not that easy, Judy. I don't really understand it, but I know it's very hard for him. He needs our prayers. He needs help, too, but that's something he'll have to ask for. I hope he can do it, for Clara's sake." Ma looked so sad right then; I gave her a hug and didn't press her any further. I went into the living room with Roy and listened to

136

the end of *The Lone Ranger*. Pa had left that morning on his boat, and we were all missing him.

The news came on and Roy went upstairs. I sat on the sofa, thinking. I was getting pretty irritated with Annette and her stupid plan—phase one *and* phase two. I decided I was going to take care of things my own way. I looked at the clock. It was late for a school night, but I quietly slid out the door and headed for Jacob's house.

I knocked on his door and waited. Jacob poked his head out. "Judy?"

"I know it's late, Jacob, but I really need to talk to you."

Jacob looked up and down the block. "What is it?" he said.

"Can we sit down?" I pointed to the stoop and motioned for him to join me. He parked himself about two feet away.

"What's going on, Jacob? I need to know."

"What do you mean?" His voice was flat and distant.

"Oh, come on, you know what I mean. You barely even talk to me anymore."

Jacob shook his head and frowned. "I've just had a lot on my mind lately."

"Well, why don't you talk to me about it? Maybe I can help."

"No one can help."

"I know you're having problems with your parents, Jacob, and if you're worried about Douglas, I'm—"

"I'm not worried about Douglas."

"Okay. It's just that ever since Charlie came around—"

"Look, I don't want to talk about this, all right?" Jacob looked up and down the street again. He was getting very agitated.

"What is it, Jacob? Are you afraid Charlie is gonna see us together? Are you embarrassed to be with me?" Heat was rising to my face, and my heart hammered.

"No, that's not it."

"So, what is it, then? Did you forget about the summer? It wasn't that long ago."

Jacob looked into my eyes. His face was so different I barely recognized him. "Maybe we need to forget about the summer, Judy. Maybe we both need to move on."

His words hurt so bad, I could hardly breathe. I stood up. Don't cry, I told myself. Don't let him see you cry.

I shook my head slowly. "I don't ever want to talk to you again." I walked down the stairs, clutching the banister. I thought maybe Jacob would stop me and say, "No, Judy, please don't go." But he didn't. I heard his front door close, and then I knew it was over.

twenty-three
just memories

When I saw Jacob at school the next day, he was trailing alongside Charlie. I knew he saw me, but he pretended not to. That's what people do—turn their backs on you, I thought. Just when you start to believe you can count on someone, they walk away like they never knew you. I decided to do more than not speak to him. For me, Jacob would not exist.

That afternoon, I went to Ma and Pa and asked them if I could still take art classes with Mrs. Marshall.

"Of course," Ma said, smiling. "I think that's a wonderful idea."

"They're not too expensive?" I asked Pa.

He shook his head. "I've set aside money just for that, Judy. It's all there."

So the next day, I went to see Mrs. Marshall and I began her first class: pencil and charcoal sketching. From then on, I went one afternoon a week, drawing and painting in various media.

Over the next few months I found ways to fill all the hours in my day, so there was no time or energy to do much thinking. Besides the art classes, I studied hard and got straight A's for the first marking period. Annette and I joined the track team, and we won the city championship for our school. I also started going to Junior League, our church's youth group, on Friday nights. Annette, Harold, and Olaf went, too.

Our youth leader, Alan, was a lot of fun, kind of like a big, goofy kid himself. He let me and Annette play on the church basketball team (there was no girls' team, of course) even though the pastor's wife thought that was just dreadful. On the weekends he took us bowling or ice skating, and sometimes we went out for pizza. Alan could be serious, too, and he talked with us about things we were going through, but I never let on about what was really happening inside me.

On those Friday nights when we walked to church, we'd see Jacob, Charlie, and their group of friends hanging out in front of the candy store or the ice cream parlor. Jacob always looked down when he saw us coming. One time I saw him smoking a cigarette, and he tried to hide it as we passed by. Harold would make a point of saying hello to Jacob, but then he'd say to the rest of us, "I don't understand that kid . . . I used to really like that kid . . . What happened to that kid?" Annette would say, "He misses Andy," and I could tell from the look in her eyes that she was missing Andy, too. She'd shown me every letter she'd got from him, and she had read them so many times, the pages had gotten soft and worn.

In school, Jacob was failing both history and English. When our history teacher handed back our first exam, he said to Jacob, "You're starting off on the wrong foot, Mr. Jacobsen." When our English teacher asked Jacob to read part of *Romeo and Juliet* aloud, he slipped farther down in his seat and said, "I don't want to." The teacher said, "Fine, that's a failing grade for oral participation." Jacob just shrugged. I knew he was hurting deep down, but I shut myself off to him. I tried to erase all the memories of our summer together.

Ma kept pestering me to invite Jacob to dinner, and she couldn't understand why I refused. When I tried to explain it to her, she shook her head and said, "That just doesn't sound like Jacob." I knew Mrs. Jacobsen was still sick, because Ma visited her during the week, carrying big piles of food. I wondered if Jacob's father was still drinking. I thought about asking Ma, but then I decided not to.

Roy whined about how much he missed Jacob, because Jacob had dropped out of Boy Scouts and never came around to see him. One time I saw Roy sitting on his bed, holding something in each hand. In one hand was the pinewood derby car that Jacob had helped him build, and in the other hand was the stuffed turtle that Jacob had won at Coney Island. He was holding them and crying.

I did my best to forget about Jacob, but sometimes at night when I was drifting off to sleep, my mind wandered back to the summer. I saw us together on that tire swing, looking over the flowers and the pond. I saw him at the spillway, leading me down that cliff with the water splashing all around. I felt his warm kiss and the trembling inside me. I saw him with his arms stretched out to the mountains and the sun shining on his face. But those were all just memories. In the morning I rebuilt the wall that shut him out of my life.

twenty-four
the date

As the months rolled by, my body started to change. My hairpin figure softened and rounded out. I was finally catching up with the other girls my age. Once, when Pa came home from a three-week voyage on his tugboat, he pretended not to recognize me. "Where's Judy?" he said, looking straight at me. For a split second I thought he was serious, and it scared me.

The next time Pa came home, I had cut my hair, and I thought he was going to break down and cry. It was shoulder length, and it fell in waves around my face. Pa told me I looked so pretty, but he felt like he'd lost his little girl. Pa was right—the cut made me look much older, and I liked it. Ma bought me new clothes, and I actually filled them out. I knew Jacob saw the change, because I would catch him staring at me in class.

When my fourteenth birthday arrived, it landed on the same day as our church Christmas banquet. The banquet was for the junior- and senior-high kids. It was actually just a regular old dinner in the church basement, but you had to get dressed up for it.

Pa said, "See, Judy, we really know how to throw you a party." That's the way my birthday was; it always blended in with Christmas one way or another. It was never a separate, distinct day.

Ma was driving me crazy, making last-minute alterations on my dress. "Stand still," she said as she tucked, pinned, and pulled.

"Ma, it's fine the way it is. *Please* let me go now," I said. I was getting fed up.

She was holding a bunch of straight pins between her lips, and when she talked she blew out the side of her mouth. "I want you to look nice, that's all. Did you know Jacob is going to the banquet tonight?"

"No, I didn't. Who told you that?"

"His mother. She was so happy about it, too. He hasn't gone to church in a long time, so try to make him feel welcome tonight, Judy. His mother doesn't like the boys he's been hanging around with."

"Ma! You don't understand. Jacob is *not* my friend anymore. I cannot make him feel welcome. He doesn't even say hello to me. He treats me like an enemy."

Ma took the pins out of her mouth and said, "That just doesn't sound like Jacob."

The finished dress was beautiful—a deep green velvet that matched my eyes, snug enough to show off my new curves. Ma let me use a touch of makeup, and she gave me a gold necklace to wear. "You *are* pretty," I whispered to myself in the mirror. I imagined what Jacob's face would look like when he saw me, but then reminded myself that I didn't care.

"Whoa!" Pa said as I walked down the stairs. "I'm not letting you out of the house like that. All those boys are gonna be chasing you."

"Pa, cut it out," I said.

"Judy has a date," Roy said. He jumped off the sofa and spun around the room.

"I do not! Where'd you get a crazy idea like that?"

"From Harold," he said. "Yesterday he asked me what color dress you were going to wear."

"Harold? What are you talking about? Harold never asked me to the banquet." I looked at Pa, and he was chuckling to himself. Ma was standing there shrugging. The doorbell rang. I walked to the door in a huff and opened it, expecting to see Annette. It was Harold, and he was holding a small box.

"Wow, Judy," he said. "You look great." I stood with my mouth hanging open. He handed me the box. "Happy birthday. It's something for you to wear tonight."

"Harold . . . I . . . I . . ."

"Go ahead, open it . . . please." I took the box from his hands, and opened it with a feeling of doom. Inside was a corsage of white orchids with green ribbons that matched my dress. A cold blast of air hit me.

"Judy!" Pa called from the living room. "Ask Harold to come in and close the door. It's freezing."

"Uh, come on in, Harold," I said.

"Hello, Harold," Ma greeted him. "You look cold. I'll get you something warm to drink."

Harold sat down on the sofa with Pa and listened to the radio. I scooted into the kitchen with Roy at my heels. "See?" Roy whispered. "I told you so. Annette has a date, too. Olaf asked me what color dress she was wearing tonight."

"Why didn't you tell me this sooner? I could have done something about it."

"Harold and Olaf gave me a dime to keep my mouth shut," he said. "Sorry."

"Roy, how could you?"

"I'll split the money with you. Five cents apiece."

I wanted to pound him. "Keep your stupid dime!" I waved him away, completely disgusted.

Ma was putting some water on to boil. I held the corsage out to her and whined like a ninny. "What am I supposed to do now?"

"I'll help you pin it on, Judy, but I have to get this hot tea ready first."

"That's not what I mean! I never agreed to go to this banquet with Harold!"

"Well, I guess you kind of have to go with him now," Ma said, looking at the corsage.

The front doorbell rang again; this time it was Annette and Olaf. Ma invited them in for tea. Annette had a funny look on her face, and as she took off her coat, I saw something pinned to her navy blue dress. It was a corsage of white orchids with navy blue ribbons.

Annette and I parked at one of the banquet tables. It was a buffet-style dinner, and Harold and Olaf were still getting their food. The place was packed; it looked like Alan had invited every teenager in Bay Ridge. Annette was buttering a roll, but she looked like she was stabbing it to death. "*Man,* I wanted to tell him off," she said, "but my mother wouldn't let me. Imagine! Me on a date with Olaf!"

"What are we going to do?" I said. "Everyone's gonna think the wrong thing."

"I don't know, but I sure want to rip these stupid flowers off my dress." Annette bit into her mangled roll. "It's embarrassing. Did you notice, no one else is wearing a corsage." I looked around the room. Annette was right. Even the girls with *real* dates weren't wearing corsages. "You know, if Andy were here, the four of us would still be together."

"What do you mean?"

"Andy and me. And you and Jacob."

"Oh, I don't know about that. You and Andy for sure, but forget about me and Jacob."

Harold and Olaf returned with heaping plates and plopped themselves next to us. I thought they looked silly all dressed up with starched collars and ties; I was used to seeing them in dungarees and T-shirts.

They shoveled food into their mouths and Annette glared at them. "There's something I don't understand," she said, tapping her fingers. "You guys know that Judy likes Jacob and I like Andy, and just because they're not here right now—"

"Olaf knows that you and Andy are still together," Harold said. "Right, Olaf?"

Olaf nodded, then swallowed his food. "Yeah, it's just a friendly date. I mean, it's not even a date, it's just . . ." He waved his hand around.

"A kind of get-together," Harold said. "And okay, if you have to know, me and Olaf would like to be more than just friends with the two of you."

"Well, that's not happening," Annette said.

Harold looked at me. "Jacob hasn't been coming around anymore and, well, I thought we could give it a try. It's working out so far, isn't it?"

I sat there stunned. I turned to Annette and she looked like she was ready to slam them both. But then, from the corner of my eye, I saw Jacob, Charlie, and a bunch of their friends stroll through the door. I pulled on her sleeve. "Look who walked in," I whispered in her ear.

"Wow," Annette said. "I'm surprised they came."

Harold and Olaf saw them, too. "Alan invited everyone," Olaf said. "You think they'd say no to free food and dessert?" He laughed and lifted a forkful of mashed potatoes to his mouth.

Harold was sort of pressed up against me, and I felt trapped. "Excuse me," I said, getting up from the table. "I just need to go to the ladies' room."

Inside the bathroom, I took some deep breaths, trying to calm myself down. Just stay clear of Harold, I told myself, and maybe no one will notice. I smoothed out my dress, but the corsage made it bunch up around my shoulder. "That's it!" I said, pulling out the pins. "I'm not wearing this thing." I flung open the door and heard a thud. I peered around the side of the door and saw Jacob hunched over, rubbing his head. "What are you *doing*?' I snapped. "Are you following me or something?"

"What am *I* doing? You're the one who just hit me with the door," Jacob said. "I was just going to the men's room."

"Well, you should be more careful."

Jacob looked at the corsage in my hand and grinned. "So, what's with the flowers?"

"For your information—it's my birthday." I felt my cheeks burning up, so I turned and walked away. Back at the table, I scooted my chair as close to Annette as possible. I wanted to disappear.

When Jacob came back from the bathroom, he walked over to Alan and whispered something in his ear. They walked out of the room together and were gone for about ten minutes. I couldn't figure it out. What could they possibly be doing? When Jacob came back, he planted himself next to a girl at his table. She pushed her chair close to his and batted her eyelashes.

Alan stood at the head table and spoke into a microphone. "Can I have everyone's attention!" His voice boomed across the room. "I've been told that we have a birthday girl among us tonight."

My head started to spin. I looked at Jacob, and as our eyes met he smiled and shrugged. I gave him a death stare as I heard my name announced over clapping and whistling. What a downright despicable thing to do, I thought.

"Hey, Harold," Charlie called out. "How'd you get so lucky tonight? A date with the *birthday girl*." That really set everyone off laughing, whistling, and clapping.

"Enough, Charlie," Alan said.

After everyone sang "Happy Birthday" to me, Alan came over to our table. "I'm sorry, Judy. I didn't mean to embarrass you."

"It's okay, Alan." I tried to smile, but the corners of my mouth wouldn't turn up.

"You're a good sport." He patted my back and went up for dessert.

"Judy," Harold said. "Do you want me to punch out Charlie after this thing is over?"

"No, Harold. Just forget about it."

"Well, here, let me help you pin these flowers back on your dress."

One thing I could say for sure: My fourteenth birthday was certainly a separate and distinct day.

twenty-five
bliss park

I'm not sure how I made it through the next week. The teasing at school was unbearable. One morning when I walked into English class, a big heart was drawn on the blackboard with the words JUDY AND HAROLD 4-EVER written inside it. Harold's friend Johnny was pointing at me and laughing, so I knew he did it. When the teacher came in, she caught me erasing the board. "But, Mrs. Polito," I said, "you don't understand. I'm—"

"You know you're not supposed to be out of your seat, Judy. Don't let this happen again."

I glanced at Jacob. He was slouched in his chair, pretending to look at a book, but I could have sworn there was a smirk on his face. That night I had to write an essay on proper classroom behavior.

Jacob was absent for the rest of the week, but I saw him in the afternoons, hanging around the candy store and smoking cigarettes with his friends. I figured if he kept it up, he'd flunk ninth grade. It would serve him right.

The first snowfall of winter came on Friday. As Annette and I walked home from school, the snow began to stick to the ground. We twirled along the sidewalks, tasted snowflakes, and breathed out big puffs of steam. The sky was the color of pewter, and the heaviness of the clouds promised a big snowfall. There would be sledding in Bliss Park that weekend.

A loud gargling sound woke me Saturday morning. I stumbled into the hallway and heard it coming from the bathroom. "Roy, what are you doing, drowning in there?" I said. I knocked on the door and tried to turn the handle, but it was locked.

"Go away," he said.

"No, I won't go away. Open it or I'll go get Ma."

Roy opened the door, and in his hand was a container of salt. "I'm just gargling with salt water, that's all."

"Why?"

"My throat's a little sore. I want to go sledding with you today, so I'm trying to get better. Don't tell Ma."

"Well, you'd better hide the salt and gargle quietly or she'll know something's up," I said.

"Okay. Promise you won't tell."

"Fine, I promise."

The whole gang of us from Fifty-sixth Street set out for Bliss Park with our sleds. The winter sun was high in the sky, and it warmed the tops of our heads as we trotted along. Roy coughed and wiped his nose with his mitten the whole time. At the park we flew down each hill, and we finished with Dead Man's Peak. By that time the sun was falling and the wind kicked up; it was cold. My wet dungarees clung to me, and my legs felt like needles were jabbing into them. I looked around for Roy and spotted him at the top of a hill with Pauley.

"Come on, Roy!" I called. "Let's go home." My teeth were chattering. Roy flew down the hill, and as he got off his sled he coughed, deep and painful. His face was pale, and his eyes were glazed over. I pressed my hand to his forehead; it was on fire. I asked Harold and Olaf to carry our sleds as I raced home with Roy on my back. I felt sick inside. It was all my fault.

Roy's fever was 105 degrees. Ma gave him some aspirin and bathed him with a washcloth. I cried and blubbered about it being my fault, and begged Ma's forgiveness. She just told me to shush. I sat by Roy's bed all night, and I must have fallen asleep, because the next thing I knew it was 5 A.M. Ma woke me and said she was taking Roy to the hospital. She was afraid to drive in the snow, so Tante Anna and Uncle John were coming over with their car.

"I'm going with you," I said. Ma was too tired to argue.

The doctor told us Roy had pneumonia.

He lay on the hospital bed in a tent-sized gown, his

bony arms and legs thrashing around with fever and chills. He whimpered as the nurse gave him shots of penicillin in his teeny rear end. He coughed so hard it made my lungs ache. Ma started shaking when he coughed up spots of blood that splattered his pillow. One nurse put Roy in a misty oxygen tent and another tried to calm Ma down, but it was no use. "Pa," she cried. "I need Pa."

Pa was on his tugboat, and I started feeling angry with him for not being there. Most of all I was angry with myself. And afraid. I was afraid Roy was going to die, and if he did, I would be to blame. Ma called for Tante Anna, but the nurses wouldn't let her or Uncle John into the room. They had to wait for us in the lobby.

Ma knelt down next to Roy, sobbing and praying. Her face looked pale, and there were dark smudges under her eyes. Her hands shook. She'd lost a child—my sister—to pneumonia before and I knew she was remembering. I thought about Ma on that boat, twelve years ago, holding my sick little sister and watching her die. I wondered if Ma had been angry because my real father wasn't there, or if she had just been sad and afraid. I sat down on a chair next to Roy's bed.

Then I felt a tap on my shoulder. It was Tante Anna; she'd gotten past the nurses at the front desk and slipped into the room. "Shhh," she said, putting her finger to her lips. I was hoping she'd hug me, but she went and wrapped her arms around Ma, and Ma cried into her shoulder. I felt like I couldn't breathe, so I got up and walked out into the hall, straining to fill my lungs with air. Then I stood at the door and listened.

"God's punishing me, Anna," Ma said. "It's pneumonia. I can't go through this. Not again."

Tante Anna shushed her. "No, Hulda, God is not punishing you. Things happen; children get sick. And it was *not* your fault with little Pearl; you know that. They have good medicine now, and Roy is going to be okay. I just talked to the doctor."

Ma buried her face in her hands. Now I knew she blamed herself for my sister's death. Was that part of the reason she had kept it a secret from me?

I spoke up. "Shouldn't we try to reach Pa? Shouldn't he know?"

There was silence for a minute; then Tante Anna said, "I suppose we could ask the men at the boatyard to contact him, but what good would it do? He can't turn the tug around and come home. Besides, there's no reason to get him all worried." Ma nodded her head in agreement.

All worried? I thought. Shouldn't he worry? What if Roy *was* dying? Would Pa just keep sailing off into the blue?

I sat by Roy's bed all night, passing in and out of sleep, wishing for someone to hold me and tell me everything would be okay.

twenty-six

rice pudding and potato pancakes

It was morning. Roy opened his eyes and found himself in the hospital bed. "I want Pa," he cried softly, rubbing his eyes. I was sitting right beside him, and Ma was asleep on the chair next to us.

"Roy, shhh. Try to calm down," I whispered. "Pa's out on the boat. We'll see him soon." I took his hand, put my mouth to his ear, and very quietly sang him a song. I wanted Ma to be able to sleep. She'd been up an awful long time.

Roy pulled himself up slowly, and I propped some pillows behind his back. He was so weak, even this simple motion was difficult. I gave him a sip of water, and then he leaned back.

"Judy," he said. "Do you think Jacob will come and see me?" His chest rattled when he breathed.

Just the thought of Jacob made my body tense up, but I tried not to show this to Roy. "Oh, I don't know," I said. "You'll be out of here soon, so let's not think about it now. Are you hungry?" I quickly opened the breakfast tray that the nurse had brought in.

"It smells bad," Roy said.

I searched the tray and found some red Jell-O. "How about this?"

Roy frowned. "I guess."

Roy managed to swallow a few bites of Jell-O, but then he felt tired again. I laid him back down. "Try to sleep," I said. Roy closed his eyes, but he was restless. He was warm with fever, and every few minutes he coughed and moaned. Again, he asked for Pa and then Jacob.

Ma woke up when the nurse came in to take Roy's temperature. "His fever's down a bit," the nurse said. "One-oh-one point five."

Ma nodded and thanked the nurse. Then she turned to me. "Judy," she said, glancing at the food on the breakfast tray, "I need you to go home and pack some things." She waited until the nurse had walked out of the room. "Roy needs something good to eat. There's lefse in the icebox—please wrap four or five and bring them here." She looked down at her dress. "And I could use a change of clothes—some underwear, too, and my toothbrush."

"Okay, Ma," I said. "I'll be back as soon as I can."

"And eat something yourself, Judy."

"I will."

I headed out of the hospital and walked along the streets; a group of people passed me, laughing and smiling, and I didn't see how anything could be funny right then. When I got to Fifty-sixth Street, I saw Annette, Harold, and Olaf building a snowman on Annette's porch. As I approached, they fired a line of snowballs at me. "Cut it out, you idiots!" I said. "Roy's in the hospital with pneumonia." Annette jumped off her stoop and dashed over to me. As we walked to my house, I told her what had happened. "And for some reason he keeps asking for Jacob. He's driving me crazy."

"Well, how about if I come to the hospital tonight to visit?" Annette said.

"I don't think they'll let you in. You're not family."

"Sure I am. You'll see—I'll be there."

Annette came to the hospital that night. She came with Jacob. Ma had gone to the cafeteria for a cup of coffee, and I was slumped in a chair next to Roy. He was asleep. When I saw Jacob, I stood up and said, "What are *you* doing here? Annette, why did you bring him?"

"Judy, I didn't," she started to say, but I cut her off.

"Jacob, I think you better leave now."

Roy woke up. "Jacob, is that you?" he said, trying to lift his head. "I knew you'd come."

Jacob and Annette sat down on Roy's bed and spoke in whispers while I paced. After a few minutes, Jacob said, "Roy, just rest now. I'll be back tomorrow."

Annette stayed with Roy, and I followed Jacob out the

door. "Just who do you think you are?" I said. "You come here like you've been part of our lives all along. You're not welcome here." I heaved with anger.

"Judy . . . I'm—"

"Go away!" I screamed.

Annette came into the hall. "Judy, calm down," she pleaded.

"No! I won't calm down." I looked at Jacob. "I'm not gonna let you hurt Roy like you hurt me. You pretended to be my friend, but as soon as Charlie came around, it was like I didn't even exist. But that wasn't enough, was it? You had to humiliate me in front of all those people at the banquet!"

"Judy, it wasn't—"

"I saw you whispering in Alan's ear, telling him it was my birthday. You and your stupid friends had a great time laughing at me, didn't you?"

"Judy, stop," Annette said.

"You're a big phony," I said. "Don't you ever come near my family again. Stay away from Roy. I hate you!" I choked on those last words and ran back into the room. I tried to hide my face from Roy. After a few minutes, Annette came in and sat by my side. "Why did you bring him here?" I asked.

"I didn't bring him," she said.

"What do you mean?"

"I met Jacob in the lobby downstairs. He was visiting his mother. He asked me why I was here, so I told him about Roy, and he wanted to come. Judy, he just found out that his mother has cancer. She might die." My head started to swim. "And I was the one who told Alan it was your birthday,"

Annette went on. "I'm sorry. I didn't know it was going to turn out like that."

When Roy came home, I didn't know what day it was or how much time had passed. The hospital had muddied my brain. Ma said it had been a week. Roy was better, but he'd lost so much weight he looked like a freckled bag of bones. Ma was determined to fatten him up with rice pudding and potato pancakes. "Good Norwegian stick-to-the-ribs food," she said as she stirred the gloppy mixture. Pa still wasn't home, and I pictured him having a good old time on the tugboat while Ma and I worried ourselves sick over Roy.

On my first day back to school, I looked at Jacob's empty seat in history class and came up with a million reasons to hate him: He's a two-faced double-crosser, a phony, a backstabber, a two-timer. The list went on and on. But I kept thinking about Mrs. Jacobsen being so sick, and I felt ashamed of the things I had said to Jacob.

When I came home from school that afternoon, I galloped up the stairs to see Roy. He was propped up in bed, reading a Superman comic book. "Hey, Roy, how ya feelin'? Had enough of that rice pudding?" I winked at him and held up a bag from the Italian bakery. Inside was a big sprinkle cookie—Roy's favorite.

"Thanks, Judy, but I'm stuffed," he said. "Jacob brought me a frankfurter and French fries from Nathan's."

"He what?" I sat down on the bed and wrinkled up my forehead. "You mean he went all the way to Coney Island just to get you that?"

"Uh-huh. Jacob and I are pals."

"Right," I said. I took out the sprinkle cookie, bit into it, and stared into space.

"Judy?" Roy looked at me with big, sad cow eyes. "Please make up with Jacob. Please be friends again."

"Roy, it's not that easy; you don't understand."

"But he told me he's awful sorry for treating you so bad."

"He did?"

"Yeah. And he said you hate him, but I told him that can't be true."

My chest sank to my stomach. "I don't hate him," I mumbled.

"Good," Roy said with a small contented grin. He held up the comic book. "Now, will you read me *Superman*? Some of the words are too hard for me."

"Sure."

Later that afternoon, I went to Jacob's house. I knocked on his door and held my breath. Jacob opened it slowly, and I could see he had been crying. "Judy? I didn't expect to see you." He stood there, not knowing what to do.

"Is it all right if I come in?" I said.

"Yeah, sure." The house was dark and quiet. Jacob and I sat down on the sofa. He started to rub his forehead. "Judy,

I'm sorry. I've made a mess of everything. We were friends, and I ruined it all."

I wasn't sure what to say; I scrunched my lips around for a while. "Jacob . . . those things I said to you . . . in the hospital . . ."

Jacob shook his head. "Oh, forget it, Judy."

"No, I can't forget it. I didn't mean it. I was angry."

"It's okay."

There was silence for a minute. "How is your mother doing?" I asked.

Jacob sighed and shook his head. "She's really sick. The doctors say she might die."

"I heard that," I said softly. "Annette told me."

"It's so bad, Judy. She can't even eat. It's real hard to see her like that." Jacob's hands were shaking. "I can't lose her," he said.

I leaned toward him, and he hung his head. I couldn't think of anything to say.

"I've lost everyone," he said. "Andy's gone, and I've lost you, too."

I sat there for a while, blinking away tears and swallowing until I found my voice. "You haven't lost me, Jacob," I said, taking his hand. "I'm right here."

twenty-seven
puke on the bathroom floor

Pa came home the next day. It was a good thing, because Ma said she had aged ten years in the two weeks before. Pa held her close, and she buried her face in his chest. He carried her to bed, kissed her nose, and tucked her in. It was Saturday afternoon, and I've never known Ma to take a nap, but she did, and Pa made lunch for us.

Roy sat on Pa's lap while we ate, and told him all about his time in the hospital. I sat feeling neglected and sorry for myself. I stared at my sandwich.

"And this mean, ugly old nurse gave me a shot in my behind with a needle this long!" Roy said, holding out both hands. "And I didn't even cry."

"Yes, you did," I mumbled. Roy made it sound like the needle he got was as long and thick as a screwdriver. Pa played along, marveling at his bravery. I was still angry with Pa for not being there when we needed him, and I acted like a cold fish.

"Judy," Pa said, "thank you for helping Ma. She told me she couldn't have made it without you."

"Sure," I said. Then I left the table and went to my room without touching my sandwich. Pa left me alone for a while, and then he came upstairs.

"Judy," he said, knocking on my door. "Can I come in?" I didn't answer. He opened the door a crack and peeked in. "Please, tell me what's wrong."

"Go away," I said.

He walked in. "Judy, I wish I could have been home. I feel terrible about not being there for Roy. I know you've been through an awful lot, too."

I looked at Pa and said, "If *I* was dying, you probably wouldn't even show up for my funeral." It was a wicked thing to say; I knew that. Pa was about the sweetest man who ever walked the face of the earth, and here I was, causing him all kinds of misery. But I wanted to hurt him.

Pa stood there for a minute. Then he lowered his eyes, walked out, and closed the door.

I moped around in bed for a while, and then I went to Annette's house. She was outside on the stoop talking to Harold and Olaf. She'd told them about Jacob's mother being in the hospital and how upset Jacob was.

Harold scrunched up his face like he was thinking real hard. "I gotta admit," he said, glancing at me, "sometimes I'd like to forget about that kid. But I guess we gotta help him out. He's been a jerk lately, but now I understand why."

Olaf nodded. "What can we do?" he said.

I thought for a while. "Well, he's failing all his classes. Maybe we could help him catch up with his work so he doesn't flunk ninth grade."

"All right," Harold said. "Let's do that."

The four of us headed over to Fifty-second Street and called for Jacob. When he heard our plan, he thanked us and said he'd really like our help. The next day was Sunday, so we said we'd meet him at his house in the afternoon. I would help Jacob with English and history, Annette would take care of algebra, and Harold and Olaf would be in charge of science.

On Sunday afternoon, I decided to go out a little early. I wanted to spend some time with Jacob before everyone else arrived. It was a warm winter day; the snow was melting and the air smelled soggy. I hauled my bike out from the garage, dusted off the cobwebs, and pedaled to Jacob's house. I didn't have to wear a jacket, and the wind felt good as it blew through my hair. Jacob was outside on his stoop with a tiny calico kitten perched on his lap. It had a big black spot over its nose.

"Oh my gosh!" I said. I jumped off my bike and ran up the steps. "It looks exactly like Bingo! Where'd you get him?"

"He was in the house when we came home from

165

church. My sister Ingrid thinks he got in through an open window. Isn't it amazing? He's got the same nose." The kitten purred and snuggled his head into Jacob's jacket.

We went inside. "Well, well," Ingrid said, smiling. "One of Jacob's private tutors come to call. Goodness knows, Jacob might have had to repeat kindergarten if it wasn't for you and your friends, Judy." Jacob ignored her comment, stretched out on the floor, and watched the kitten pounce on a ball of paper. Jacob's other sister, Aslaug, brought the kitten a saucer of milk, and as he lapped it up, the front door opened and Mr. Jacobsen walked in.

"I have some good news," he said as he hung up his hat. "Ma will be able to come home for Christmas."

"Oh, Pa!" Aslaug cried. "That *is* good news."

The kitten scampered across the room, chasing a button. Mr. Jacobsen scooped him up and rubbed his head. "So, Jacob, what do you think of your new kitten?"

"Huh?" Jacob said.

Ingrid laughed. "You mean *you* brought him home, Pa? All this time we thought he sneaked in through a window."

Jacob scowled and when his father handed him the kitten, he turned away. "Jacob!" Ingrid said. "What's wrong with you?"

Jacob stood up and marched to the front door. He turned and looked at his father. "You think you can make everything right just by giving me a cat, do you? I wish *you* were the one with cancer. I wish *you* were the one who was gonna die!" He walked out the door.

"Jacob!" Ingrid screamed.

"Ingrid, don't," Mr. Jacobsen said. "Let him be."

I slid out the door. Jacob was sitting on the stoop, hunched over, his head in his hands. I sat down next to him. "Jacob, your father is trying real hard to make things right." I felt like a big hypocrite saying that after the awful way I'd treated Pa.

Jacob looked up at me. "I don't believe a word he says anymore. Now my sisters tell me he stopped drinking again, but who knows how long that'll last? And it's only because my mother's sick. If she wasn't sick, he'd still be doin' the same old thing. He never even said he was sorry for killing Bingo. Never said he was sorry for anything."

"People have different ways of saying they're sorry. Maybe for him, getting that kitten is *his* way."

"It's too late," he said.

Mr. Jacobsen stepped quietly onto the porch and sat down next to Jacob. I got up to leave, but Mr. Jacobsen motioned for me to stay. "Jacob," he said, "I know I've failed you in so many ways. I wish I could take Ma's place. I wish it was me that was sick." He sighed and his face looked old and tired. "I've made a promise to your mother that I'm not going to drink anymore. I know it's hard for you to believe me, but things are different now. There are some men at church who are going to help me, keep me accountable. I'm making this promise to you, too."

Jacob looked at the ground. The kitten leaped out the door and brushed up against his leg. Mr. Jacobsen continued. "I want to ask you to forgive me, Jacob, for everything."

I really started feeling out of place, because at that moment, Mr. Jacobsen put his hands to his face and started crying. I didn't know what to do. I remembered the handkerchief that Ma always made me carry in my pocket; I reached in and pulled it out. "Thank you, Judy," he said, taking it to dry his eyes. Then he turned to Jacob. "I hope you'll keep the kitten, Jacob."

There was a tense moment of silence. Jacob stared straight ahead and didn't respond. After a while, his father gave up and walked back into the house.

A few days later, we all got together at my house to study, and Jacob brought the kitten with him. I was glad he'd decided to keep it.

There was something on my mind that day, and I couldn't concentrate on our schoolwork. "Jacob," I said, "I need to ask you a question."

"Okay, shoot."

"At the Christmas banquet, what were you whispering in Alan's ear, and why did the two of you leave the room for about ten minutes?"

"Oh, that? I told Alan that some kid puked all over the bathroom floor. Then I helped him clean it up." Harold, Olaf, and Annette thought that was hysterical, and they laughed like hyenas.

"Yuck," I said, crinkling my nose.

"Hey, Jacob," Harold said. "I got a question, too. What

are you gonna do about that windbag friend of yours—Charlie?" Everyone went silent.

Jacob stuck his pencil behind his ear and scratched his head for a while. "Well," he said, "a couple of weeks ago, Charlie asked me to sneak some whiskey from my house. I told him that my father didn't keep liquor in the house, which is true, and that he only drank at bars. I said, 'Even if he did, I wouldn't get it for you.' Then Charlie told me I was good for nothing. He told me not to come around anymore. I said, 'No problem—I wasn't planning to anyway.'"

We were all shocked at the way Jacob said this so matter-of-factly. We sat with our mouths hanging open. Then Harold turned to Olaf and said, "Let's pummel that kid Charlie tomorrow. I'll get my brother, Steve, and we'll take care of him and his friends. He's been asking for it for a long time."

"No," Jacob said. "Don't do that."

Harold looked at him, puzzled.

"There's been enough fighting, Harold," Jacob said. "And it never does any good."

Harold crunched his eyebrows together and thought for a while.

"Jacob's right," Olaf said.

Harold looked at all of us. "Oh, okay," he said. "I still think Charlie's beggin' for a black eye, but fine, no more fighting."

twenty-eight
peach-pit rings

"Jacob, it's your girlfriend!" Ingrid called when I arrived at their door on the morning of Christmas Eve. Then she noticed Roy standing next to me. "My, oh my," she said, smiling. "Judy, I knew you had a brother, but you never told me he was *this* handsome. Come in, come in." I thought Roy was going to faint from happiness.

Jacob was sitting on the living room floor with his cat; his mother was on the sofa. She was gray and skeleton-like, but she smiled when she saw me and Roy.

I was holding two Christmas gifts. One was a box of Norwegian cookies that Ma had baked—*krum kake* cones, spiced with cardamom. I handed them to Mrs. Jacobsen and sat down. "My mother's coming to visit tomorrow," I told her. "And just to warn you, she's bringing a bunch of food."

"That sounds like Hulda," Mrs. Jacobsen said, smiling.

Ingrid sat down with us, and Roy climbed into her lap. "Are you married?" Roy asked her.

Ingrid laughed and bounced him on her knee. "Yes, I am."

I shook my head and gave Roy a warning look that meant he'd better behave. Then I handed Jacob the other gift. "Thanks," he said. "I have something for you, too. Come on upstairs and I'll show you." He took me into his room. On one wall was a bookcase filled with books. He picked one out and handed it to me.

"*The Grapes of Wrath?*" I asked.

"No, silly. Open it up." Inside the book were pages and pages of pressed flowers and butterflies. "They're from the summer. I pressed every kind of wildflower I could find. And I didn't kill the butterflies. They were already dead when I flattened them out." As I flipped through the pages, I felt a burst of warmth, like I was walking through those familiar fields again.

"There's something else," Jacob said, opening his drawer and taking out a teeny box. He handed it to me. Inside were three small wooden rings, smooth and shiny, with dark little grooves. "I made those from peach pits— from Mrs. Breuger's tree. I sanded them down and drilled out the middles."

171

I slipped one on my finger and smiled at him. "They're beautiful," I said. "Thank you." Then I pointed to the gift I'd brought. "Now it's your turn."

Jacob opened the box and pulled out a bag of rock candy. His face lit up. "It's perfect," he said. "We both gave each other gifts from the summer."

"There's more," I said. "Look underneath." He carefully pulled out a piece of paper underneath the rock candy. It was a sketch I'd made of our most secret place in the Catskills—the place with the tire swing and the big old bathtub—the place where he had kissed me and carved our names into the oak tree.

He held it to the light and studied it carefully. "Judy, this is *really* good."

I blushed. I knew it was good. Mrs. Marshall told me it was the best piece I'd ever done. Jacob put the picture down on the bed. He slid his arms around my waist and kissed me. "Thank you," he said.

When we went downstairs, Jacob's father was waiting for us in the living room. He was sitting on the sofa, holding three small presents. "I have early Christmas presents for all three of you," he said. "Roy, I want you to open yours first." He held one box out to Roy.

"Oh, boy! Thanks!" Roy hopped off Ingrid's lap and opened the box. It was a rabbit's foot.

"That's for good luck," Mr. Jacobsen said.

"Wow!" Roy said. He rubbed the rabbit's foot. "I always wanted one of these."

Mr. Jacobsen handed me a long, thin box. Inside was a rosebud carved out of wood. It had a delicate stem, and there were even small thorns on it. "Thank you," I said. "I've never seen anything like it. It's beautiful."

Mr. Jacobsen's face crinkled with a smile. Then he held a box out to Jacob. "Jacob, this one's for you."

Jacob didn't move.

"Please take it, Jacob," he said.

Roy couldn't figure out what was going on, and he desperately wanted to see what was in the box. He took the gift from Mr. Jacobsen and handed it to Jacob. "Jacob," Roy said, "don't you want to see what you got?"

Jacob frowned; then he tousled Roy's hair. "Sure, Roy. Here, let's see what's inside." He opened it. Inside was a pocketknife.

"Wow!" Roy said. "What a great gift."

Jacob rolled the knife around in his hands, and then he opened the blade. He looked at his father. "Thank you. It's a good knife." His eyes were watery, and he looked down at the knife again.

His father said, "If you like, Jacob, I can show you some things about wood carving. Whenever you're ready, that is. Just let me know."

twenty-nine
our precious pearl

There was something I had to do.

I carted Roy home and found Pa in the living room fiddling with his Santa suit; the rest of the house seemed empty. I walked into the kitchen and came back out.

"Where's Ma?" I said. "She didn't leave for Tante Anna's already, did she?"

"Yes," Pa said. "Tante Anna called and asked her to come a little early. She needed some help with the cooking and baking. Ma wants us to come over around two o'clock."

"Oh," I said, plunking down onto the sofa.

"When do we open the presents?" Roy said.

Pa laughed. "After we eat dinner—and no pestering

174

this year. You need to mind your manners at Tante Anna's house."

"Okay, okay," Roy said. "Can I go call for Pauley now? He doesn't celebrate till tomorrow."

"If it's all right with his mother," Pa said, "but don't be long."

Roy ran out the door, and Pa turned to me. "How is Mrs. Jacobsen?" he asked. "Did she like the *krum kake*?"

"She did," I said. "She seems happy to be home."

Pa sighed. "I'm glad they let her out of the hospital for Christmas." He paused for a moment, then held up his Santa suit and smoothed out the wrinkles.

I sat there quietly, thinking, my heart beating fast and my stomach fluttering. If Christmas was going to feel right this year, I had to do something. I wanted to talk to Ma, but now she wasn't here.

Pa picked up the long white beard. "This thing has seen better days," he said, smiling and shaking his head.

I glanced at him, but I wasn't paying much attention to what he was doing. Then I thought maybe it would be better to ask Pa what I needed to know. That way I wouldn't have to upset Ma on Christmas Eve.

"What do you think, Judy?" Pa put the beard to his chin and made a funny face. I didn't laugh. "Judy?" he said, peering at me. "Is there something wrong?"

I could barely breathe. Pa came and sat next to me. "What is it?"

I didn't speak right away. Then I forced the words from my mouth. "Where's my real father?"

175

Pa looked at me for a while, stunned. Then he said, "We're not sure, Judy. We think he died."

I thought about my dream of the faceless man walking deeper and deeper into the ground. "I should have known," I said. I blinked back tears and told myself I was glad he was dead, but a big pain welled up inside me.

"You should talk to Ma," Pa said. "She can tell you more."

I shook my head. "I don't want to upset her today." Then I looked at Pa. "I just wanted Christmas to be the same this year. I wanted to feel normal again."

"I can understand that," he said.

"Can you tell me something, Pa? I want to know—is my sister buried somewhere? Did Ma take her body off that boat?"

"Yes, Judy. She's buried here in Brooklyn, close to where Tante Anna lives."

I thought about that. Ma lived with Tante Anna when she first came to America. It made sense that my sister would be buried close by; that way Ma could have walked there. "I know it sounds crazy, Pa," I said, "but I want to visit her grave today, before we celebrate Christmas."

"Oh, I don't know," Pa said, shaking his head. "You and Ma should go together. Not today, but soon."

"I want to go alone," I said. "It's important to me, Pa. I can take the trolley if you just tell me where the grave is."

Pa watched me with a pained expression. "If you really have to go, Judy, I can drive you there."

176

"But I want to do this on my own, Pa. It's not that far, and I can easily take the trolley."

Pa argued a little longer, but when he saw how determined I was and how much it meant to me, he gave in.

I rode the trolley and then walked to the small graveyard next to the old Lutheran church. It didn't take long to find the headstone.

OUR PRECIOUS PEARL
DAUGHTER OF ANDERS AND HULDA ANDERSEN,
NOVEMBER 13, 1931—MAY 10, 1932
WE LOVE YOU, MAMA, PAPA, AND SISTER, JUDY

I stared at the inscription and knelt down because my knees were shaking and I thought I'd topple over. Such a short little life, I thought.

I took off my gloves and slid my hands over the inscription. Anders—that wasn't Pa's name. It had to be my real father's name. But why did it say that? How could my father have loved little Pearl? He left us, and probably drank himself to death. I sat there for a long time, wondering. Then I heard footsteps behind me.

Ma knelt down next to me and put her arm around my shoulder. "Pa called me," she said. "I didn't want you to be here alone."

The two of us were quiet for a minute; all I heard was my own breathing as it made a cloud of steam in the cold air.

"I'm so sorry, Judy," Ma said. "All along I thought I was protecting you, but now I can see—I was protecting myself, too. I was afraid to tell you about your father, and I felt so guilty about what happened to Pearl."

I didn't understand that. "But there was nothing you could have done, Ma. She got sick. I heard what Tante Anna said at the hospital. It wasn't your fault."

"I blamed myself for taking her on that boat," Ma said. "Pearl was so tiny—just a little thing—and I was desperate to leave." Ma touched the gravestone; her hands were shaking.

"It's okay, Ma," I said. "You don't have to say any more if it hurts too bad."

"No," she said. "There's more I have to tell you." She took a deep breath and let it out slowly. "Your real father—Anders—he was a good man; I want you to know that. He had a younger brother, Hans, and they worked together on a big fishing boat off the coast of Norway. There was a very bad storm, and Hans was thrown off the side of the boat. Your father dove in and tried to save him, but the ocean was so rough—the worst storm they'd ever seen." Ma paused for a moment and looked at me. "Your father was never the same after that. He blamed himself for Hans's death, and that's when he started drinking." Ma lowered her eyes. I put my arms around her.

"There's more, Judy," she said. "He wasn't drunk the day he died; he was completely sober. That morning he gave you a big hug and stroked your hair; then he kissed the top of little Pearl's head. He said to me, 'I'm sorry for being such a failure.' I didn't say anything because I was angry with him for letting liquor control his life. He went out on that same fishing boat, and we never saw him after that. The crew couldn't explain it. 'He disappeared,' they said. And all I kept thinking was one thing: Why didn't I just throw my arms around him and tell him I loved him before he left?"

This was all too much for me. I felt weak and dizzy. "You mean, he . . ." I couldn't get the words out.

"No one knows for sure, Judy. They never found his body. It's an awful thing, and I was so afraid to tell you." There were tears on Ma's cheeks. We sat there a little longer, and Ma started shivering. "It's cold," she said. "We should go."

"I need to stay, Ma. I need to be alone and think."

Ma's face looked so sad. I knew she didn't want to leave me, but after a while she agreed. "Okay," she said, "but before I go, there's something else you need to know. It's important and I want you to listen carefully."

I felt a little frightened. "Okay," I said.

"When I came to America after losing Pearl, I went into a severe depression. Do you know what that means?"

"Like what happened to Andy's mother?" I said.

"Yes, something like that. It was very scary. I was living with Tante Anna and Uncle John, and they didn't know what to do. At that time Uncle John was captain of his tugboat, and Pa was his mate. They became good friends, and since Pa was single and very lonely, he spent a lot of evenings at their house. When he came to visit, I always hid away in my room, but you just loved to see him. He'd walk in the house and say, 'Where's my Judy?' and you'd go running. You'd sit on his lap and play the whole night." Ma stopped for a minute and took my hand. "You see, Pa fell in love with you first—before he even knew me. And then, when I started to get better, Pa was the one who made me smile again."

My chin began to quiver, and I couldn't keep the tears from rolling down my face. Ma hugged me. "I know you want to stay a little longer, Judy, but please come to Tante Anna's soon. It's so cold."

"I think I have to go home first—to our house—when I'm finished here," I said.

Ma nodded slowly. "Okay, then." She pulled off her hat and scarf and put them on me; then I watched her walk away.

After Ma left I cried some more. Everything was like a jumbled-up puzzle, and I needed to put the pieces together. I thought for a long time. Maybe my father fell off that boat. Maybe it was an accident. But maybe it wasn't.

I thought about how I'd felt when Roy was sick in the hospital, and how I'd blamed myself for it. What if Roy had died? Would I ever have forgiven myself? I thought about Andy's mother, holding that ice pick in her hands and blaming herself for what had happened to Andy. And then I thought about Ma and how she had blamed herself for what happened to little Pearl.

I was sad for my real father, and I wished he had been stronger than his pain. But I couldn't blame him. I had to forgive him.

On the way home I thought about what Ma had said—about Pa loving me before he loved her. When I walked in the house, Pa was sitting on the sofa dressed in his Santa suit. He seemed to be waiting for me. I ran to him and we held each other for a long time.

thirty

a better place

Over the next few months, Mrs. Jacobsen was in and out of the hospital. It was very hard on Jacob and his family. By April, the doctors sent her home with just a short time to live.

On April twelfth, we heard over the radio that President Roosevelt had died. He'd suffered a massive stroke. We all stood in the living room in a state of shock. "Who's the president now?" I said.

Pa looked at me. "Truman."

"Who's Truman?" Roosevelt had been president my whole life. I didn't know anyone else.

Ma lowered herself to the sofa. "Now the war will never end," she said.

Pa put his arm around her. "It will end," he said. "It must."

We listened to the radio every day. U.S. troops were pressing into Germany. Hitler's army was growing weaker. Then we heard Eisenhower's account of the death camps across Germany. The murder, starvation, and torture of the Jews. I couldn't believe it. It was so awful that Ma would not let Roy listen; she sent him out of the living room whenever the news came on. All along, it had never been quite clear to me why we were fighting this war. But now I knew for certain what we were fighting against.

A few weeks later, President Truman made an announcement over the radio:

"This is a solemn but glorious hour . . . General Eisenhower informs me that the forces of Germany have surrendered to the United Nations."

It was V-E Day—Victory in Europe. Soldiers began pouring back into the States, and Ingrid and Aslaug got their husbands back. The war in the Pacific was still going on, but Peter was able to come home. They all moved in with Jacob, and that house was bursting at the seams with people. Mrs. Jacobsen had her whole family together under one roof. Ma said it was God's perfect timing. He'd given Mrs. Jacobsen a chance to see each one of her children before He took her home. And Mr. Jacobsen kept his promise—he didn't drink again.

• • •

Jacob's mother died one morning in May, when the roses were beginning to bloom. After the funeral service, Jacob asked if I would ride with his family to the burial. That turned out to be the hardest part for Jacob, because it was so final. He placed a bunch of roses on top of his mother's casket before they lowered it into the ground. We knew she was in a better place.

After the funeral, Jacob stayed in his room for a few days and slept most of the time. Ma said it would take a while before his tears ran out. She said we needed to be patient with him, help him get through it one day at a time.

Annette, Harold, Olaf, and I continued to help Jacob with his schoolwork, and when we went to Junior League on Friday nights, we dragged him along. He didn't participate much, but I think he enjoyed being with us. Sometimes at night, I'd call for him and we'd take walks together.

One day, toward the end of June, I pedaled my bike down Fifty-second Street and saw Jacob and his father sitting together on their front porch. They were carving away at some wood, and the black-nosed kitten, Bingo #2, was batting around the wood chips. I parked my bike and hopped up the steps.

"Judy," Mr. Jacobsen said. "Come and take this boy away from the house. He needs to run around, play some ball, have a little fun."

"Okay," I said. I looked closely at the small wooden figures sitting on the bench next to them. "What are you two carving?"

"It's Noah's ark, with all the animals," Jacob said. "It's going to be for Ingrid's baby. She's pregnant."

"Really?" Suddenly I felt happy. Soon a baby would be running around their house. "Well, do you want to go, Jacob? Everyone's waiting. We're gonna play some stickball."

"Sure," he said, putting down his knife. Then he turned to his father. "I'll be back later, Pa. Then we can finish."

Mr. Jacobsen smiled and waved us away. "Go have fun."

Jacob took my hand, and we ran down the steps. I hopped onto the handlebars of my bike and he pedaled the two of us to Fifty-sixth Street. When we played ball that afternoon, he slammed a home run, and for a few seconds a smile spread across his face.

On the last day of school, Jacob came running toward me, waving his report card in the air. "Judy! I passed everything!"

He handed me the paper, and I scanned the grades: C in algebra, C in English, and B's in the rest, except for an A in science.

"An A in *science*?" I moaned, and handed the paper back to him. Harold and Olaf were the ones who'd tutored Jacob in science. "Gosh, we're never gonna hear the end of it from Harold."

Jacob smiled and stuffed the report card in his pocket.

"Hey, I have a great idea," he said. "Let's get everyone together and go to the ice cream parlor—my treat. My father gave me two dollars yesterday and it's still in my pocket."

"Okay, but it doesn't have to be your treat," I said.

"Yeah, it does. You guys helped me so much. I probably would have flunked ninth grade if wasn't for you. Let me treat. I want to."

So Jacob bought us milk shakes and French fries, and we toasted his report card. I was right about Harold. He kept looking at the report card and saying, "An A in science—see that, Olaf?" Then he looked at the rest of us and grinned. "Don't see no other A's here."

Annette snatched the report card and glared at him. "Give it up, Harold."

Halfway through July, Annette got a letter from Andy. He was coming home. That week we watched a moving truck come and cart off Charlie's stuff. "Good riddance," Harold said. "Hope we never have to lay eyes on that kid again. Maybe we'll get lucky and he'll move to the Bronx."

On the day Andy was to return, we all sat on Jacob's stoop and waited. A big truck barreled up the street, and I caught a glimpse of Annette—her eyes grew big, and she squeezed her kneecaps. Jacob bolted toward the truck and ran alongside it. When the truck stopped and Andy hopped out, the two of them flung their arms around each other.

Andy's brothers jumped off the back, whooping and hollering. Their mother got out and scolded them, but she couldn't help laughing; she looked so happy to be home. Then we all gave Andy a big hug. He hugged Annette extra long and whispered something in her ear that made her blush.

Andy told Jacob how sorry he was about Jacob's mother, and how he wished he could have been there for him. Jacob said not to worry; he was just glad Andy was back home.

A man was there with Andy and his family, and at first I thought he was the truck driver. He helped Andy's mother with the boxes and suitcases, but then he put his arm around her and she smiled at him. I wondered who he was, and I wondered if Andy minded him doing that. But then I thought about Pa and how he had helped Ma come out of her sadness. I wondered if this man might be doing the same for Andy's mother.

Andy looked so different I could hardly believe it. He'd grown about a foot taller, and his shoulders were a mile wide. He kept looking at us, saying how much we had changed. I guess we had. I guess we all changed a lot that year.

thirty-one

the waterfall

We all wanted Jacob to share our little bungalow in the Catskills that summer. It wasn't that he didn't want to come; he said Peter and his father needed him more. Since school had let out, the three of them had been going fishing together for days at a time. And since Peter was going to college in the fall, Jacob wanted to spend as much time with him as he could.

A few days before our vacation, I took Jacob to the place where little Pearl was buried. I was finally ready to tell him about Pearl and about my real father. It hurt all over again, but having Jacob there with me felt good.

I'd brought some flowers, and Jacob helped me plant

them around the headstone. We sat down in the grass, and he asked me if Roy knew about Pearl. "No, I haven't told Roy anything," I said. Then I realized I wanted to protect Roy, just like Ma had wanted to protect me. And then I understood everything a whole lot better. I understood how hard it had been for Ma to tell me about my father and Pearl.

After we sat there for a while, Jacob got real quiet. "I wish my mother was still here," he said. "I miss her."

I put my arms around him, and we held each other. When it was time to leave, we walked home, holding hands. His hand felt warm and right inside mine, and I wanted to keep walking like that forever.

I brought Roy to Pearl's grave the next day. After I told him the story, I said, "So I'm really your half sister."

Roy looked at me like I was crazy. Then he hugged me and said, "You'll always be my whole sister." He got on his knees and ran his hand over the inscription. "I wish we could have known her, Judy—our sister, Pearl."

"Me too, Roy." I knelt down next to him, and for the first time in a long while, I felt like Roy's whole sister. Then I thought of something. "I have a picture of her," I said. "Ma gave it to me. I'll show it to you when we get home."

I was cranky on the first of August, the day we left for the Catskills. I wanted Jacob to be with us. Roy slept the whole way, and Ma and Pa were busy discussing a new washing machine and maybe a new car now that the war was almost over. I was lonely. Even our lunch at the Red Apple didn't cheer me up. The shrimp salad sandwich felt like glue in my mouth, and I couldn't finish it.

Mrs. Breuger greeted us with the biggest prune-face smile I'd ever seen. Her grandsons were staying with her for the summer. They were doing repairs on her house and fixing up her property. "Where is Jacob?" she asked me.

"He's not coming this year," I said, fighting back the tears. Mrs. Breuger nodded like she understood.

After we'd unloaded the car, Ma chased us out of the house so she could disinfect the place. Roy ran to Billy's, Pa went out back to the hammock, and I knew where I had to go. I secretly set out for the five-mile walk to the spillway. I couldn't tell Ma where I was going, because she didn't allow us there. I felt bad and hoped she wouldn't worry, but I had to do it. I was so restless inside.

As I walked along the road, the country air made me feel better. I smiled, remembering when Jacob had first breathed it in and thought it was wonderful. When I reached the reservoir, I hiked through the woods to the clearing of streams and bedrock; not a soul was there. It was strange being all alone with the big blue sky and the mountains. I sat down on a rock and looked at the water splashing and crashing around the edge of the cliff. I was scared, but I walked to the edge and began to climb down. When I reached the bottom, I dove into that deep, dark pool of water. I hopped onto the rock where Jacob and I had once sat together—where he had first kissed me.

My clothes clung to me and the breeze blew, but I wasn't cold; I was looking for something. There it was. The waterfall I remembered—the one Jacob called our waterfall. The sun was still shining through it, making a rainbow. For some reason I had to make sure it was still there. So much had changed in the past year, but I was beginning to see that some things never changed: the way my parents loved me, and the way Roy called me his whole sister, and the way Jacob's heart was connected to mine.

It turned out to be a great summer. I visited Mrs. Breuger a lot, and Pa let me drive the car all by myself when we went into town. I sketched and painted almost every day, and at the lake I learned how to do jackknives and one-and-a-halfs off the diving board. I spent time with Audrey and laughed while she flirted with the lifeguards. I picked and pressed wildflowers and ate lots of rock candy. Jacob and I exchanged many letters. I signed mine *xoxo, Judy*. He signed his *J&J 4Ever*.

While we were away in the Catskills, the United States dropped two atomic bombs on Japan—one on Hiroshima and the other on Nagasaki—and Japan surrendered. August fifteenth was V-J Day—Victory in Japan. The war was finally over.

When we got home to Brooklyn, there were block parties going on in our neighborhood almost every night of the week. There was music, dancing, food—everyone was celebrating. Bunches of soldiers and sailors were returning home. The whole gang of us—me, Jacob, Annette, Andy, Harold, and Olaf—stayed out late on those summer nights. We walked the streets, listened to the music, and watched the young men in their uniforms jitterbug with all the pretty girls. When Fifty-sixth Street had its very own block party, Jacob twirled me to the music, and Andy did the same with Annette. Harold and Olaf grabbed some girls and we all started to jitterbug together. Ma came out the door, and I said, "Uh-oh," but she just smiled and waved.

author's note

Dancing in the Streets of Brooklyn is a story that comes from my imagination, but it is also mixed with the memories of my childhood and the stories passed down to me by my parents and grandparents. The characters are fictional, but some of them are loosely based on real people in my family.

Like Judy and Jacob, my parents grew up in the Norwegian community of Bay Ridge, Brooklyn, in the 1940s. They experienced World War II on the home front. This was a time of great patriotism and self-sacrifice. They enjoyed simple pleasures like games of stickball with their friends, swimming in the Sunset Park pool, and trips to Coney Island. My mother had a younger brother with a fantastic imagination, much like Roy. My parents knew each other from a very young age and later became high school sweethearts.

In 1944, Bay Ridge was home to many ethnic groups—mostly Irish, Italian, and Scandinavian. The section of Eighth Avenue that ran from Fiftieth to Sixtieth Street was sometimes referred to as Lapskaus Boulevard, named after a thick Norwegian stew. By the time I was a young girl, the neighborhood had become more diverse, but there was still a large Norwegian core. Every year we celebrated our heritage with a parade on the seventeenth of May—the day Norway gained independence from Sweden. We marched along the streets in our Norwegian costumes, waving Norwegian flags.

My grandparents lived on Fifty-sixth Street, and every Sunday after church we went to their house for a midday meal. Like Ma, my grandmother often cooked Norwegian meatballs, my favorite. Like Pa, both my father and grandfather were tugboat captains. When I was eight years old, my mother took a job with *The Norway Times,* a small Norwegian newspaper based in Brooklyn. I liked to visit her office and watch how fast she could type.

If you take a walk down Lapskaus Boulevard today, you will see something completely different. The area has become the home of one of the largest Chinese populations in the country. The streets are still full of festivity, just as they were in 1944, and the people who live there now are celebrating their heritage in a new and ever-changing way.

acknowledgments

I would like to thank my editor, Françoise Bui, for starting me on this incredible path and then giving so generously of her warmth and talent; my agent, Laura Rennert, for her counsel and encouragement; my parents, Alf and June Andersen, for sharing their memories and never tiring of my continual flow of questions; my uncle Roy, for being such a good sport; my children, Elizabeth, Daniel, Jonny, and Korina, for providing a daily source of inspiration; and most of all, my husband, Ed, my very honest first reader, my best friend.

about the author

April Lurie was born and raised in Bay Ridge, Brooklyn. She is the granddaughter of Norwegian immigrants. As a girl, she enjoyed playing ball with her friends in the neighborhood, taking walks to the candy store, and riding the Cyclone at Coney Island. She graduated from Hunter College/Bellevue School of Nursing in Manhattan and worked as a neonatal ICU nurse at Maimonides Medical Center for ten years. April Lurie now lives in a noisy house in Round Rock, Texas, with her husband, four children, and two dogs. She maintains her sanity through writing. This is her first novel.